SOMETHING LIKE HAPPY

Something Like Happy

JOHN BURNSIDE

JONATHAN CAPE
LONDON

Published by Jonathan Cape 2013

2 4 6 8 10 9 7 5 3 1

Copyright © John Burnside 2013

John Burnside has asserted his right
under the Copyright, Designs and Patents Act 1988
to be identified as the author of this work

Portions of this work have appeared previously in other publications

First published in Great Britain in 2013 by Jonathan Cape
Random House, 20 Vauxhall Bridge Road, London SW1V 2SA

www.vintage-books.co.uk

Addresses for companies within The Random House Group Limited
can be found at: www.randomhouse.co.uk/offices.htm

The Random House Group Limited Reg. No. 954009

A CIP catalogue record for this book is available from the British Library

ISBN 9780224097031

The Random House Group Limited supports The Forest Stewardship
Council (FSC®), the leading international forest certification organisation.
Our books carrying the FSC label are printed on FSC® certified paper. FSC is the
only forest certification scheme endorsed by the leading environmental organisations,
including Greenpeace. Our paper procurement policy can be
found at www.randomhouse.co.uk/environment

Typeset in Bembo by Palimpsest Book Production Limited,
Falkirk, Stirlingshire

Printed in Great Britain by
Clays Ltd, St Ives plc

CONTENTS

SOMETHING LIKE HAPPY

The first time I saw Arthur McKechnie, he came into the bank with some cheques. I had just started working there, fresh out of school and a bit nervous, I suppose, and I liked the way he behaved, all polite and nicely spoken, which was more than I could have said for some of the other customers. By the end of that first, almost wordless transaction, I had already decided he was someone I could have liked, but I had also noticed that he was a bit *too* different, one of those men who thinks too much about stuff that nobody else bothers with, or he doesn't pay enough attention to other people to understand what they might do, when push comes to shove. As he stood there with the pen in his hand, very obviously reading the badge pinned to my lapel, I found myself wanting to shake him out of the little dream he was in.

Of course, I noticed the name the moment he handed over the paying-in slip. Arthur McKechnie. Everybody knew the McKechnies, and most people knew they were a bad lot, but I knew them mainly because my sister Marie was going out with the worst of them. People would tell Marie that Stan McKechnie wasn't right for her, which was a mistake, because all that opposition only made her more determined to stick with him. Besides, Stan was good-looking, if you didn't study him too closely. Not like this Arthur, who seemed put together from a kit, all angles and mess, with an odd cast to the eyes and a mouth that didn't look altogether finished, like the mouth in a kid's drawing. I didn't know then that he was Stan's little brother. Marie had never mentioned an Arthur, though she talked about the McKechnie sisters all the time. We all did. Some people thought the McKechnie girls were even worse than their brother, if only because they were nice-looking and dressed smart and, if you didn't know them from old, you didn't see what they were capable of until it was too late. With Stan, you knew what he was at first sight; it didn't matter how well he scrubbed up. There was a meanness in his face that you couldn't miss, unless you were Marie and wanted to miss it.

Arthur didn't say much. He handed over the money and the paying-in slip; then, when I had processed the transaction, he took the confirmation chit and, carefully, making no attempt to hide what he was doing, wrote down on the back what it said on my lapel badge. He was a slow writer. He held his pen in an odd way, between the first two fingers of his left hand, and he angled his arm round to make the letters, writing them out large: 'FIONA, TRAINEE'. He didn't seem to care that I could see what he was doing. When he was done, he looked up and nodded.

'Is there anything else I can help you with today?' I asked, not sure whether I was amused or annoyed.

He shook his head. His voice, when he talked, was soft. 'Not today, thanks,' he said, with an odd, even suggestive emphasis on 'today'. He smiled then; it was a tight, secretive kind of smile, but it wasn't mean, and I could see that he didn't think there was anything out of the ordinary in what he had just done. He wasn't being smart, or impolite. He'd just written my name on the back of his confirmation slip, the way a child would do, for reasons of his own that had nothing to do with anybody else.

I wanted to say something, but I couldn't find the right words. I just shook my head ever so slightly and looked out to the line for the next customer – and Arthur McKechnie turned to go, that odd little smile on his face, a smile that I could see even then was the sign not only

4

of a secret happiness but also of his inevitable fall. I'm not saying I knew what that fall would be, or claiming it was some kind of premonition; God knows human beings are made for falling, and most human beings in that town were going to fall sooner rather than later. But I did see something out of the ordinary, and I'm sorry now that I didn't take more notice.

I asked Marie about Arthur when I got home that night. She was preoccupied, getting ready to go out with Stan, so I thought she'd just shrug it off, but she stopped putting on her make-up and sat looking at me through the mirror, her eyeliner suspended in midair.

'Arthur?' she said. 'Where did you come across *him*, for God's sake?'

'He came into the bank today,' I said.

'Oh, yeah?' Her hand dropped and she grimaced. 'Well, don't be getting interested in *him*. Stan says he's a nutter.'

'So who is he, then?' I said, picking up some clothes that were scattered around the place. I was always clearing up after Marie, even now, when we didn't share a room any more.

'He's Stan's brother, of course,' she said. 'He's really pissed Stan off, though.'

'Oh.' I folded her powder-blue sweater and put it away in the chest of drawers. 'Why's that?'

'Something to do with money,' she said. She watched as I gathered up a pile of obvious laundry. 'Why? You're not really *interested* are you?'

I snorted. 'Of course not,' I said. 'I just don't remember you ever mentioning that Stan had a brother.'

'Yeah, well.' A worried look crossed her face. 'There's not much to talk about. I hardly noticed him at first. He's hardly ever there when I go round. When he is, he just sits in a corner, reading.' The thought of it made her shiver. 'Stan's old man says Arthur's not a real McKechnie.

5

He says Margaret must have got him from some tinker woman she met outside the off-licence.' She started working on her make-up again. 'It might even be true, for all I know. I mean, he's nothing like Stan.'

'So why is Stan annoyed with him?'

Marie shook her head. 'Search me,' she said. 'Anyway, I've got to hurry. I'm going to be late.'

I studied her as she applied the finishing touches to her face. She wasn't pretty, but she tried hard. She had been working for three years at the biscuit factory and, though she would never have admitted it, she was jealous of me, having a good job at the bank. For her, that meant I had a future. Of course, I couldn't tell her that a future didn't mean as much to me as she thought it did. It *was* a good job and everybody said I should be grateful; most girls from my background ended up with no prospects, just eight hours a day on the packing line. People were always saying how lucky I was, as if I had won the lottery or something. 'Where are you going, anyway?' I asked.

She stood up and gave a little twirl. 'No idea,' she said. 'I don't think Stan's got any money.'

'Well,' I said. 'Maybe he should ask Arthur for a loan.' I smiled sweetly.

'Ha-ha,' she said. 'Very funny.'

Marie had never thought much of me, or my taste, when it came to matters of the heart. It was probably fair to say that I was better-looking, and the teachers at school had always referred to me as the smart one, but it's no big secret that, with boys, giving out the right signals matters more than looks or brains. Just before then, I'd been going out with a boy called Jack, but when it didn't work out I felt an odd relief, like someone who had been rescued from the need to maintain some minor but time-consuming pretence. I wasn't like Marie. She had always liked the idea of love; even at nine, she'd had a boyfriend, a kid called Tony Ross who gave her cards at Christmas and on her birthday. All through her early teens, she had very obviously *liked* boys, and they had liked her, mostly because boys like to be liked. For Marie, intelligence in a boyfriend was the worst kind of liability, and the few boys I did bring home knew how to write their own names and do basic arithmetic, at the very least. Which was more than anybody could say for Stan, and this was one of the reasons that my father got so angry with Marie a few days later, before he left for his shift at the works.

'Stan McKechnie will never amount to anything,' he said, in his customary, quiet but final style. 'He can't keep a job, he doesn't know how to handle money, he wants something for nothing. Someday he'll find out that the world doesn't owe him a living. You steer clear of him, you hear?'

Marie always seemed genuinely surprised that people thought so ill of Stan; after all, she would say, the McKechnies weren't the worst people on the estate, not by a long way. Stan had been unlucky: his mum had died when he was at a vulnerable age, and his sisters had spoiled him rotten. His dad was a bit of a rogue, everybody knew that, a rogue with a liking for the bottle, but Stan was doing the best he could, and he had big plans. He just needed a break, that was all. Of course, it was sad listening to her talk like that, and I'm not sure she even convinced herself much of the time. The fact was that after she chose Stan she couldn't have let go, even if she wanted to. She didn't want to have to admit she had made a mistake; she couldn't be seen to give in to pressure. Even when the rumour about Bobby Curran started going around, she refused to believe that Stan was involved.

'People shouldn't spread stories,' she said. 'Not unless they know all the facts.'

The facts, it turned out, were fairly straightforward. Bobby Curran had been drinking in the White Swan when Vincent Cronin and his brothers had come by. There had been bad blood between Vincent and Bobby since the previous winter, when they'd got into a drunken argument about a motorcycle at a Christmas party. Everybody knew the affair wasn't over, but nothing happened until that night in the Swan, six months later, when they found Bobby alone and half-cut in a place where he hardly ever drank. The Cronins were too scared of Bobby to have a square go with him; even that night, when it was three against one, they didn't do anything right away, because none of them was carrying. They couldn't have fought it out with fists and boots, like in the old days – they had to be armed. Since Vincent lived right across the road, all that was needed was someone to keep an eye on Bobby so he didn't leave, and the Cronins would run back to Vincent's flat for some blades. Stan was the one who kept Bobby talking while the boys got themselves ready. Then, when Bobby went out back to the toilets, he gave the Cronins the signal and they went in.

It was over in seconds: Bobby probably didn't even know what hit him. The Cronins ran out, their clothes covered in blood, but nobody tried to stop them. Jim the landlord came around the bar and went out the back to see what had happened, and he did first aid on Bobby while somebody called the police and most of his custom melted away, not wanting to be there when the law arrived. The only one who stayed put was Stan McKechnie. He watched the police come in, and he watched the body being taken out, and he never batted an eyelid. Nobody knows who spread it about that he'd been involved, and nobody could say for sure that the story was true, but everybody believed it – which meant that it didn't matter whether it was true or not.

It was a summer of hard, yellowish heat. The air was never quite clear anyway, because of the works, but this year it was thick and dry, like a fine material wrapped around my face and arms. The bank was supposed to be air-conditioned, but the system didn't really work; by the end of the day, I was desperate to get out to somewhere cool and wash away the thick gauze of heat on my skin. Sometimes I just went home and showered, then sat by a half-open window waiting for the night, Marie out on the town with Stan, my parents on back shift at the works or sitting downstairs watching game shows. But now and again I would go out to the old swimming hole, the place everybody called the Twenty-Two, and spend half an hour or so in the water, not really swimming so much as hanging there, suspended in the rumour of coolness that rose from the depths below.

Usually, I was alone, even though everybody knew about the place; in school, we had spent weekend afternoons out there, five or six of us going together to swim and talk and smoke cigarettes, trying out love and friendship and loneliness like teenagers in a pop song or a movie, but we always got home in time for supper, and we spent the evenings elsewhere, at clubs and discos and pubs, dressed in the clothes we thought suited us, waiting to be seen by boys we thought we liked. Nobody had ever gone swimming at the Twenty-Two in the evening, but that was the best time when the weather was hot. There was a current that flowed through the hole – a current that nobody could quite explain, some underground run or spring deep in the earth – and it was cold and quick, a near-animal force moving and turning in the water. I had always felt that, how something alive seemed to brush against my skin, coming up out of the depths to pull at my legs or encircle my feet. It wasn't just a surface motion; it was bone deep, a force with a shape of its own. Maybe it was a great hank of river weed turning below in the cold current, maybe it was just the way gravity works in water, but it felt like something that matched me exactly, the same shape and weight and volume, and it always seemed as if that something came to life the moment I stepped into the water.

On the few occasions when I met other people at the Twenty-Two, I felt cheated, as if I had looked out of the window at home and found someone having a picnic or passing a bottle back and forth on our lawn. Mostly, though, I got to be alone. I liked to get there about six-thirty or seven, when people were still having supper or watching television, and I would just slip into the water and swim around in circles, to get cool. It wasn't exercise, like swimming in a pool. I just liked being in the water and feeling that echo of myself deep down in the current, matching my every stroke, or falling still when I stopped moving. Sometimes I swam out to the middle and stayed there, treading water, listening to the quiet that surrounded me, a hiatus in the air, like a held breath. If other people came along while I was swimming, I would hear them long before they got to me, and I would just doggy-paddle over to the bank and get my stuff together so the moment wouldn't be spoiled.

I'd never seen Arthur out there. I'd never seen him anywhere other than the bank, and it was a surprise when I caught sight of him one evening coming out of the water, white and strangely angular, in a pair of pale-blue shorts, his hair plastered down over his forehead, his arms and chest glistening. I was about twenty yards away when I saw him, and before I could think it through I had ducked in among some bushes. I was hoping he hadn't noticed me, I suppose, because it was embarrassing, meeting him like that, but he'd seen me, all right. I'm pretty sure he saw me before I saw him, and he'd been watching me coming along the track, watching in complete silence, standing still in the cool water, waiting to see what would happen. I thought he *wanted* to embarrass me, just to see what I would do. That couldn't have been true, though, or not altogether true anyway, because he turned quickly and swam away as soon as he saw that I'd seen him, gliding out to the middle. He was a good swimmer, easy and lithe, like some animal that belonged to the water, some creature of trust and grace; it was only a matter of seconds before he reached the centre and dived, vanishing into the dark water, as if there were a way out down there, some exit that only he knew. One minute he was there, the next he was gone, leaving barely a ripple behind.

I didn't know what to do. I stared at the point where he had disappeared, thinking he would come up for air, curious to see if he would call out to me, or wave, or whether he would just dive again, and keep on diving, till I left. It struck me then that I would have done exactly what he was doing if the roles had been reversed. I imagine I could have stayed down there for a minute or so, maybe more. Not long enough, though.

I don't know how long Arthur stayed down, but it was more than a minute. More than five minutes, probably. I kept thinking he would have to come up soon, but he didn't. He stayed under. The thought crossed my mind that the current had caught him and dragged him away; I even imagined having to go and get help, or having to dive in and save him when he came up half-drowned and struggling for his life, but I didn't do anything. I just stood there. Maybe he had some trick, like that thing you see in old films, where the spy or whoever sits for hours underwater, breathing through a hollowed stick or a reed. Maybe he was ready to drown rather than admit defeat and come up again, feeling awkward and cheated. I didn't know, but I couldn't quite manage to believe he was in any danger, and after a while I didn't want to see his face, because I knew I had stolen a private moment from him. I wished I could have said something, maybe called out that I was leaving and he could come out now, but I didn't say a word. I just turned around and walked back the way I came, following the track up to the road, with the cool of the water hole at my back, and a sound I almost heard, like a bird taking flight off the surface of the water, or a fish breaking the calm in the first grey of the evening, leaping out into the dizzy, unfamiliar world, to snatch its prize.

The summer passed, the hot days fading into a wet, sticky autumn. I saw Arthur at the bank from time to time: sometimes he spoke, mostly he just handed over his little bundle of cheques and the paying-in slip, with the amounts made out in his neat, slightly childish handwriting, but he didn't seem as distant, or as shy, as he had when he first came in. After our encounter at the Twenty-Two, it was as if we had a secret between us, something we both knew about but had promised not to mention, and though nothing ever happened between us, I realised, come September, that I liked him a little, even if it wasn't a liking that Marie would have understood.

Somewhere between the last warmth of the summer and the damp cool of Halloween, I noticed a change in Marie, and I knew it had something to do with Stan. I didn't know at first, though, that it also had something to do with Arthur. Stan had never treated Arthur as a brother, from all accounts, but before that summer he had mostly just ignored him. As far as Stan was concerned, Arthur really was the boy in his father's joke: a scrawny kid the tinkers didn't want, sitting in a corner of the kitchen, dreaming his life away, never saying a word. Then, beginning that summer, everything changed. The first trouble had been about the money: Stan never had any, but that was no great shame till his brother started coming home with pockets full of cheques and cash from his odd jobs. What was worse was that Arthur just kept squirrelling it all away in the bank: after he'd paid for his digs – which Stan almost never did – he saved whatever was left, going

out every day with a packed lunch of peanut-butter sand-
wiches and not coming home till late, still not saying
anything, but happy in a way that Stan didn't understand,
happy, or something like it, as if he had lain awake one
night and hatched some foolproof scheme, some plan for
a future that Stan couldn't even have imagined. That went
on for several weeks, and it drove Stan crazy, but he didn't
say anything to Arthur. He just took it out on Marie,
sulking when they went out on dates to the Hearth or
the Nags. Sometimes he'd take her out, then he'd leave
her at a table with a couple of the other girls while he
went wandering around the lounge, talking to his mates
and doing deals, the way the old married men did with
their wives. He'd buy her half a lager top, then he'd be
off, playing pool with somebody Marie didn't know or
chatting to Jenny, behind the bar. He'd been out with
Jenny once, he said. Now they were just good friends.

Marie could have sat out the sulks, if that had been all
there was to it – but suddenly, with winter approaching,
Arthur changed again. First, he bought a guitar. 'A bloody
guitar,' she said. 'I mean, he doesn't even know how to
play.'

'What kind of guitar?' I said.

She looked at me as if I were part of this great conspiracy
against her happiness. 'How do I know?' she said. 'What
difference does it make?'

I shook my head. I'd noticed a change in Arthur a week
before, when he had come into the bank and, for the first
time, made a withdrawal. I wouldn't have thought much
about it, except that he didn't seem to know how to get
money out of his account. He had to ask.

'Is it an electric guitar or an acoustic is what I mean,'
I said.

Marie thought a moment. 'Acoustic,' she said. 'He just
sits there, in the front room, strumming. Stan can't stand
it. None of them can.'

'Maybe he's going to start a band,' I said.

Marie snorted. 'That'll be the day,' she said.

It turned out Arthur had no intention of starting a band. Stan asked him once, when Marie was there; it was an ugly little scene, with Stan and his dad poking fun at the younger brother while Arthur just sat at the kitchen table, stroking the guitar strings, with his head turned away toward the window. Marie said he didn't say anything – he just sat there with a sad little smile on his face as if he felt sorry for them all, though you could see he was trying not to cry. She almost felt sorry for him herself, she said, but then he'd asked for it, really, what with his stupid guitar and his weird new clothes.

I'd seen Arthur at the bank the day before, and he'd been dressed as usual, in black jeans and a navy-blue shirt. 'What clothes?' I asked her.

'Oh, God,' Marie said. 'You should see him. He's completely changed. Bright stripy shirt, this weird-looking suede jacket. At least I think it's suede.'

'When did that start?'

'Not long ago,' she said. 'He's completely different. He plays his guitar all day, then he goes out, nobody knows where. Stan's dad says he's got himself a fancy woman.'

I shook my head. I felt strangely disappointed in Arthur, maybe for doing all this stuff in front of his dad and Stan, and maybe because I could just see him with some woman, making a fool of himself. 'I don't think so,' I said. 'Not Arthur.'

Marie laughed. It was a cruel laugh. 'Oh, yes,' she said. 'He's fairly come out of his shell now he's got a bit of money.' She gave me a hard look. 'You missed your chance there,' she said.

I was annoyed then. Not with her but with myself, for getting involved in the conversation in the first place. It didn't matter to me what Arthur McKechnie did. Good luck to him, if he wanted to blow his hard-earned money on the latest fashions and a guitar he couldn't play. I looked at Marie, and I saw the little glint of nasty pleasure in her eyes. 'You going out tonight?' I asked her.

'Of course,' she said. I could see her thinking: What a stupid question.

'With Stan?'

She rolled her eyes. 'Yeah,' she said.

I nodded. 'I'm not the only one who missed my chance,' I said. I regretted saying it as soon as it was out.

Marie's face went very bare, then she laughed. 'You're pathetic,' she said, but it wasn't that convincing, and I felt even worse, not just for her, but also for myself, that I could be so petty.

We found out later that Arthur McKechnie mostly just got dressed up in his odd clothes and sat alone in a Chinese restaurant with a half-bottle of white wine and a plate of crispy fried duck. Or he would go to a church social and hide in a corner, watching the people dance. That was probably where he met Helen Walsh, and that was when the real trouble started.

It wasn't much of a story, really. It seems that when Arthur was still in primary school Stan McKechnie and Helen Walsh were in middle school together. The Walshes had lived on Devon Way, two doors along from the McKechnies, and though they were never friendly – Joe Walsh always saw himself as a cut above – Stan had decided that he and Helen were an item, trailing along to school beside her, trying to make conversation, doing stuff to impress her, acting as if they had something more in common than a street address. I don't think Helen ever took any of this seriously, but by the time he reached third year Stan was going around talking about her as his girl-friend, and he'd been upset when Joe Walsh did well and moved his family off the estate to one of those so-called executive houses with a separate dining room and French windows at the back leading on to a patio with raised beds and a walled yard. All the McKechnies had been upset, in their own way, to see the Walshes get on: Stan's dad resented Joe's success, saying he was just a brown-nose anyhow, and the sisters put it about that May Walsh had a fondness for vodka. Stan hated the Walshes more than any of them.

'Stan's not happy,' Marie told me one day after work. 'Arthur keeps taking his stuff.' She shook her head. 'Big mistake.'

'What do you mean, taking his stuff?' I couldn't imagine Arthur as a thief, and if he were I couldn't imagine Stan having anything he might want.

'Just stupid stuff,' she said. 'Clothes and stuff. He says he's borrowing it, but Stan doesn't let anybody borrow his things. Can you imagine?' I shook my head to confirm that I couldn't. 'And then he wears Stan's best shirt to go out on a date with that stuck-up Walsh bitch.'

'He didn't.'

'Oh, yes.'

'No,' I said. 'I mean, it wouldn't have been a date, would it? Can you imagine Helen with one of the McKechnies?'

Marie shot me an ugly look. 'What's that supposed to mean?' she said.

'You know what I mean,' I said. 'I'm not talking about you and Stan—'

'Yes you are,' she said. 'That's exactly what you're talking about.' She lit a cigarette. She didn't usually smoke in the house, in case Dad caught her. 'But me and Stan are happy. I don't care what Dad says. I love him and I'm going to marry him.' She sounded like a little girl in the school playground. 'And you can take a look at yourself before you start judging other people.' She turned away slightly and stood looking out of the window, with her cigarette hand pressed to her cheek.

I didn't see any point in replying to that. I wasn't

angry with her – I wasn't even upset. For a moment, I even wanted to go over and give her a hug or something, but we didn't do that kind of thing in our family. 'I'm not judging anybody,' I said, after a while. 'I just want you to be happy.'

She looked at me then, and I could see she was close to tears. 'Happy,' she said quietly, as if it were some foreign word whose meaning she couldn't quite remember. She laughed. 'Happy,' she said again. She took a draw on the cigarette, and, in the smoke and the early evening light, she looked almost pretty, like a girl in a television show on the night before she runs away from everything, written out of the script to begin a new life somewhere else.

It snowed early that year: a freak blizzard, a beautiful anomaly. It was the kind of snow you see in films, white and perfect and deep, the cars moving slowly along white roads, the people coming out of their houses in the morning or stopping on the high street to notice the light. For a while, it was as if the works didn't exist; the snow just kept falling, white upon white upon white, and nothing was grey or smoky or tainted enough to leave a lasting stain. It really was beautiful. People came into the bank in coats and gloves, brushing the snowflakes off their shoulders and hair at the door, smiling to themselves, gladdened by the brightness of the day. You could see the child in every face, a buried life rising to the surface, a lightness about the mouth and eyes, a childish sweetness returning to a dried-out voice. Everyone seemed happier, or almost everyone. Stan McKechnie wasn't happy. I would hear about it from Marie from time to time – the petty details, the black moods, the muttered threats – but I had stopped paying attention. It just seemed too ridiculous, in all that snow and light.

The snow didn't last, though. It was replaced by a grey

lull, all smoke and pig iron. So what I remember now about the day Stan McKechnie almost killed his brother is how the light changed after the snow melted. It was a day that could have happened only in a town like ours: the sun was bright, warm even, but there was a chemical haze in the air, a blurred, dusty quality to the light that we knew from having lived so long in the shadow of the works. That was what I knew about that morning, that pale haze, and the thin ferrous smell that became a taste in the mouth, part rust, part churchyard – but there was something else that day, something I hadn't felt before. If I had to describe it, I'd say it was a sense of how things must have been before any of us came to be in that place, a stubborn beauty in the light that filled the trees, a sense of the land around us, with its buried dead and winter trees, its livestock and clouds and fence posts, there before we were and treating us as an exception to the norm, an ugly but fairly minor crease in the fabric of things, irrelevant to the larger picture.

The attack happened because of Stan's black sweater. That was what people said, at least, when it was all over: 'That Stan McKechnie, he almost murdered his brother, all because of a sweater.' Marie told me about it while we were both getting ready to go out, on the night Stan and Arthur finally came to blows. That afternoon, Arthur had borrowed Stan's aftershave, then put on the new black sweater that Stan had bought the weekend before, even though Stan had told him a thousand times that he didn't want anybody touching his things. Nobody knew where Arthur had gone, but Stan had rung Marie up and told her he was going to do something about it once and for all. Marie had tried to calm him down, but she knew there was no point; Stan had been heading for a big blowout for weeks now, she said, and she knew trouble was coming. Nobody could have predicted how far it would go, and nobody would ever understand what had led up to the final moments. It would be just another story people told each other, another cautionary tale about the McKechnies, how in that family one brother could kick the other senseless over a borrowed sweater. Marie told me about it that night, all the while so wrapped up in her own worries that she didn't even notice I was getting ready to go out. Then, when she had finished talking, and I'd told her not to worry, that it would all blow over, she realised.

'You got a date?' she asked, blurting it out, not hiding her surprise.

I laughed. 'Don't sound so shocked,' I said.

'Who with?'

'None of your business,' I said.

'Oh, God!' She put her hands to her face. 'It's not Arthur, is it?'

I looked at her. She was serious, but I could see in her face that she wasn't concerned about me – she just didn't want this mess to get any bigger than it already was. I shook my head.

'It's not, is it?' she asked again. 'Please tell me it's not.'

I was tempted then to tell her it was, just to see the look on her face, but I didn't. I just shook my head again. 'Don't be daft,' I said.

It wasn't a real date, anyway. Somebody from the bank had asked me out, a tall, thin man called Peter who worked in business and foreign. He was a bit older than me, but I'd been bored and surprised when he asked, and I'd accepted his invitation to go for a drink at the Falcon before I registered what was happening. That's how it goes in the workplace. All these office romances start out of boredom and wanting something to happen to break the monotony. As things turned out, it was a pretty monotonous evening too, and I was regretting my mistake long before Arthur came into the lounge bar and stood waiting for someone to serve him. He was alone, all dressed up in Stan's black sweater and a pair of greenish trousers; maybe he was meeting somebody, maybe he was just out to see what was happening. One thing I knew for sure was that he wasn't on a date with Helen Walsh. As I sat listening to Peter going on about his plans for the future, I watched Arthur order his drink, a lager top, and it occurred to me that I didn't really know him. I told myself that it would be a mistake to get mixed up in his feud with Stan, that I really ought to mind my own business, but I was bored with Peter's supposed prospects, and I was grateful for any excuse to get away from him, if only for a few minutes. Peter didn't seem to mind when I told him there was someone I had to talk to. 'Family business,' I said, by way of explanation. He just nodded and took a sip of his beer. Maybe he was bored with me, too.

Arthur didn't see me coming. He hadn't even noticed me when he came in, or maybe he had and didn't want me to know. Maybe he was embarrassed about the Twenty-Two after all. For the first time, it occurred to me that he might have been, and when he finally turned his head and saw me I knew I was making a mistake. Only it was too late to go back. I gave him a serious look. 'Nice sweater,' I said.

He put his glass down on the bar and looked at me. He knew who I was, but he was surprised that I'd spoken. 'Thanks,' he said. 'It's not mine. I just borrowed it.'

'It suits you,' I said.

'Thanks.'

'You know Stan's looking for you,' I said. The sooner I said what I had to say, I thought, the sooner we could get away from one another.

He looked puzzled. 'Sorry?' he said; the moment he spoke, though, he worked out what I meant. He shook his head. 'Oh, no,' he said.

'Really,' I said. 'He's been building up to something for a long time.' I felt stupid: I sounded like somebody out of a soap, or a bad movie. What was I doing? None of this was any of my business. I glanced back at Peter. He had gone over to play the fruit machine. I turned back to Arthur. 'It's none of my business,' I said. 'I just thought you ought to know.'

'You've got it all wrong,' he said. 'Stan is my brother.' He studied my face. 'We're *brothers*,' he said.

'I know,' I said. I wanted to say more, but I couldn't think of anything.

For a moment, I thought Arthur was going to laugh; then, as if noticing me for the first time, as if I were some puzzle he'd been gathering clues about for weeks and had only just solved, he gave me a serious, almost concerned look. 'It's all right,' he said. 'I know you only mean well, but Stan's my brother. He knows I wouldn't do him any harm.'

I should have given up then. That would have been the sensible thing. I don't know now why I carried on. 'I don't think he does,' I said. 'He's looking for you right now.'

He smiled softly. 'How do you know that?' he asked.

'My sister told me.' I really was embarrassed to hear myself saying that, like a kid telling tales. I knew it was hopeless, and I wanted to stop talking and just take hold of him and lead him somewhere, into the shadows for safety, out to the Twenty-Two, to where he could hide under the water until the danger had passed.

'Ah.' He leaned toward me, and the light from the optics shifted on his face a little, so he looked softer, less defined. 'Marie is your sister.'

I nodded. For a moment, I thought I had got through to him – that my relationship to Marie had convinced him that I knew what I was talking about. For a moment, he put his head down and stared at the ground, and I thought he was thinking about what I had said. For a moment, maybe he was. I have no idea what went through his mind then, but when that moment had passed he was looking at me, smiling again, shaking his head almost imperceptibly. 'Thanks for your concern,' he said. 'But I'll be all right.' He put his glass down on the bar; it was still half full, but he left it there and started away. 'Honest,' he said. He seemed disappointed, for that one moment, but not with Stan. He was disappointed with me, maybe because he thought this was some game I was playing, some elaborate ruse to get his attention. That was possible. He did remember the Twenty-Two, and he'd noticed me in the bank; maybe he liked me, and my talking to him about such things had made him feel awkward. All this was going through my mind as he turned to leave, but there was something else, something that I couldn't have explained. I didn't register it then, not in words, but I think that was when I knew he was already gone and that nothing anybody could have told him would have made the least difference to what he did next. Because, for all the most ordinary, all the most banal reasons, he was doomed. He was an innocent, a lost cause, a stranger in the only place he had ever known, and he couldn't do anything about it. Under different circumstances, Arthur McKechnie would have been one of those people you read about in the newspaper: the schizoid boy who jumps out of a window thinking he can fly, the mad explorer who crosses the Arctic with nothing but a rucksack and a pair of crampons. He glanced back as he was going, and I could see that he knew as well as I did that there was nothing more to say, but he said it anyway. 'Be seeing you,' he said.

An hour later, Stan caught up with him. I'm pretty sure he didn't intend to hurt his own brother as badly as he did, not over a borrowed sweater. But then it wasn't his intentions that mattered. He's supposed to have told the police that he doesn't remember what he did that night, but there were about a dozen witnesses, and they all gave more or less the same account: Arthur had been to the Hearth, and he was walking back home when he met Stan outside the kebab place on Gloucester Road; Stan had run up, shouting and throwing punches; Arthur had just stood there, not saying anything, taking the first couple of blows as if it were some kind of game – and he had a strange look on his face, the people said, an odd half-smile that nobody could understand, though they all saw it, and they all said the same thing afterward, that it was the smile that made Stan crazy, that odd little smile that seemed to say Arthur wasn't going to take what was happening seriously, not Stan's anger or the punches raining down on him. Some of the people who saw it all said he must have been a bit simple, just to stand there grinning like that, provoking his attacker and not doing anything to defend himself.

When it was over, Stan didn't make any serious effort to get away. He stood awhile, looking around at the gang of people who had been watching it all, as if he were surprised they hadn't done anything to stop him. People said afterward that they'd thought Arthur was dead, the way he just lay there on the pavement, all twisted around and not moving. The ones who were there at the start knew they should have done something to stop it, but they all just stood watching, about eight or ten at the beginning and then more, the entire queue from the kebab shop pouring out on to the pavement to see what was going on. None of them tried to stop the attack, and nobody tried to take hold of Stan when he turned away and walked off down the road. He wasn't running; he wasn't even in a hurry. Somebody said later that he could have been out for a stroll, except that he had blood all over his coat and hands. He didn't go toward his house, he walked the other way, and he didn't stop walking until the police picked him up, an hour later. When they took him in, apparently, he told them he didn't mean it. He hadn't known what he was doing, he said. He just saw red.

After Stan was arrested, Marie wouldn't leave the house. Everybody was talking about what had happened, telling old stories about some of the bad things Stan had done in the past, about the drug dealing and breaking and entering when he was in school, or that time with the Cronins and Bobby Curran in the Swan. Some of the people who had witnessed the attack – the ones who had stood by and done nothing – were even saying Stan was getting off lightly, because he should have been up for attempted murder instead of GBH. Meanwhile, Marie stayed off work and sat in her room with the radio on, though I doubt she ever heard it. Sometimes she came downstairs, still in her pyjamas and dressing gown in the middle of the afternoon. She didn't say much, and when she did speak she would say crazy stuff. 'I wish I could just disappear,' she'd say. 'I wish the earth would just open and swallow me up.'

We all knew that something needed to be done to get her out of this depression, but nobody wanted to take the first step. So we waited. Sometimes I'd have a talk with Mum, where we would go through all the usual arguments, then one of us would say something reassuring, and we'd get on with our lives. 'It'll pass,' Mum would say. 'She's bound to be upset after all.' Or I would point out that my sister, sitting upstairs in her dressing gown, was better off, now that Stan was behind bars. 'If that's what he could do to his brother,' I would say, starting a sentence I would never need to finish, and waiting for the little grimace of horror that signalled her agreement. I'm not saying we didn't care. It was just that we didn't know what to do, and we couldn't really face the awkwardness of having to find out. Meanwhile, Marie grieved, and we went about our business, pretending there was nothing wrong.

They were probably doing much the same thing in the McKechnie household. The elder son had been locked up, and his brother was in a hospital ward; all the old man could do was sit indoors and hope the world passed him by till it found something else to talk about. Even the sisters were ashamed of what Stan had done, and they had always doted on him. I heard they all went as a family to visit Arthur in the hospital, and he wouldn't even see them. He just waited till he was well enough, then he came into the bank, withdrew all the money that was left in his account, and walked back out into the grey afternoon, to God knows where. That was the last time I saw him, the day he came for his money, and he had a dark, set look to his eyes that frightened me a little. He didn't come to my position to make the withdrawal; he waited till another cashier was free and went to her. When he'd finished the transaction, he put the money in his coat pocket and muttered something under his breath; then he left, without even a backward glance. Nobody knows where he went. The best way to think of it is that he just disappeared.

The week before Christmas, it snowed again. I had gone up to the shops, and I was walking home, crossing the park on Weymouth Road when it began, thick and fast from the moment it started falling, settling on the grass and the thin, wet shrubs around the playground. It kept falling all along the street, whiting out the gardens, lying in thick folds on the hedges, and I couldn't help but slow my pace, just to be out in all that white, watching things melt into this perpetual motion, so thick and fast by the time I got to my own front gate that I could hardly see. Everything was disappearing into the flow of it, houses and parked cars and pavement; behind me, the town was nothing but a rumour, a faint aftertaste of iron and smoke and a shadowy mass dwindling into the blizzard. At the gate, I looked back in the direction I had come from. The snow was completely different now from the snow we'd had in November: back then, it had been all brightness and visible marks, tracks and scuffs in the white turning to plum-blue and black as darkness fell, but this was dark from the first, a new variant of dark, a new form. That first snow had been the snow in a film; this was the snow in a dream.

It was bitterly cold. I hadn't noticed going out, but I felt it now, a pure cold seeping into my bones – and as the snow erased the gardens around me, I could feel this pure cold singling me out, isolating me on that street and erasing me, flake by flake, moment by moment. Marie had said she wanted to disappear, but she hadn't meant it: what she really wanted was to go back to the time before she met Stan, when life seemed full of possibilities. She didn't want to be invisible, she wanted to be seen as she saw herself, not as a character in a local news story. She wanted to be good. When she talked about disappearing, when she said she wished the earth would swallow her up, I knew that her shame wouldn't last, and it wouldn't matter much, in a year's time, what had happened to her. She would meet someone else, and she would get married and live as our mother had lived; people would think of her as somebody's wife, and then somebody's mother, and she wouldn't be invisible, ever.

But I would. I would be invisible. It was already happening, in this relentless, quick snow; I was already disappearing, and not just disappearing into that whiteness but into everything around me. Like a ghost in a film, melting into the scenery, I was starting to vanish from my life, not by going away somewhere but just by staying where I was and doing what I had always done. Working at the bank, making dinner, reading my books, swimming at the Twenty-Two

in the summer, walking in the snow in the winter. It
had something to do with Arthur, all this vanishing,
which was ridiculous, but also true. Unlike Marie, I
didn't want the earth to open and swallow me up, but
at that moment I knew I was already starting to fade
away – and it wasn't such a bad feeling, after all, to be
disappearing. It wasn't a bad thing, and maybe it was all
I had ever wanted. To stay where I was and disappear
into the wallpaper. To want nothing – not a good job,
not a husband or children. Not money or happiness.
Not what my parents would have called a future. My
entire life would be like those mornings when the
postman comes and stands at the door, sorting through
a pile of cards and letters; he thinks nobody is at home,
because the house is so quiet, but someone is in the
kitchen all the time, listening to him fumble with the
mail as she makes tea, or butters toast, not quite happy,
if you want to talk about happiness, but not unhappy,
either. It wasn't the kind of thing you see in films or
on television, but it seemed good to me, as I stood there
in the snow, vanishing imperceptibly into the life I had
not chosen but would not refuse, now that I knew what
it was.

When I got inside, I found Marie sitting in the kitchen,
watching the kettle boil. Her face was white and empty,
no make-up, her hair a mess. The windows were all misted
up, and it occurred to me that she had probably been
there awhile.

'Are you OK?' I asked.

She looked at me, but she didn't speak. She had been
in the middle of making tea, it seemed, when I came in,
but she had forgotten what she was doing, or maybe
decided that she couldn't be bothered.

'Can I get you something?' I asked.

She shook her head. 'I keep thinking about Stan,' she
said.

I nodded. 'Of course you do,' I said. I took a step closer. I thought about reaching out and touching her, on the arm, or the shoulder, then decided against it.

She laughed softly. 'It didn't suit him,' she said. 'I told him when he bought it. I said right away, when he tried it on, "It doesn't suit you, Stan."' She looked at me. 'Anyway,' she said. 'It was only a sweater.'

I nodded again. I didn't know what to say, and I wanted to cross over to her and do something, but I didn't know what. After a while, I fetched tea bags down from the cupboard, and finished making the tea. Then I put six slices of bread in the toaster. It was quiet now, no talk, no sound, only the silent continuum of snow at the window – and I wanted to make her see how beautiful it was, if not always, then at least for now, but when I turned around she was asleep in her chair, her head flopped back, her arms dangling at her sides. It was like a balancing act, something she had refined over the years, and no matter how precarious it looked I knew she would not fall. I considered taking my tea through to the sitting room, but I decided to stay and keep her company. Maybe she would wake up soon, and if she did maybe she would be hungry. That would be a good sign, I thought. It was always a good sign in books when people who had been depressed began eating again. It was the beginning of something: a new life, a recovery.

I put six more slices of bread into the toaster and fetched marmalade and a brand-new pot of blackcurrant jam from the cupboard. When it was all ready, I carried my cup and the two plates of freshly buttered toast to the table, one for her and one for me. I was hungry now, and I soon ate the portion I had made for myself, not bothering with the jam, just enjoying the taste of warm butter and crisp, fresh toast. It was delicious, like something from long ago, some childhood pleasure. Then, when I had finished that, I poured myself some tea, and because

I was still hungry, and because I really did feel happy, sitting there in the quiet, watching the snow, I sneaked first one slice, then another, then all of the toast I had made for Marie, and ate it with the jam, while it was still warm.

Slut's Hair

The tooth had been bothering her all day, and that was why she told Rob about it. She hadn't wanted to, and she knew it was a mistake telling him anything, but then everything she did these days was a mistake, and she couldn't go on forever, day and night, being careful what she said and, at the same time, not seeming to keep things from him, because that made him angrier than anything else. A wife shouldn't have secrets from her husband, he would say. If there was one thing he hated, it was secrets. He had asked her what was wrong when they were sitting down to eat, though she didn't know why, because she hadn't said a word about it. If she had, he would only have told her to stop complaining. He didn't like people who complained all the time, instead of just getting on with it. So, even though the tooth was all inflamed and throbbing by the time he got in, she'd been careful not to let on that she was hurting – and she didn't see how he could have known, because she'd kept the pain to herself, and just got on with making his dinner. But then, he was like that sometimes. It was as if he could read her mind.

'So,' he had said, out of the blue, as she brought him his Tennent's. 'What's wrong with Janice now?' She had made spaghetti again, because pasta was cheap, even though he didn't like to have the same thing too often. She reckoned if she used different sauces, like tomato one night, then maybe bacon and mushroom a couple of nights later, it wouldn't seem like too much of the same. He liked pasta, so it wasn't as bad as if it was rice, or mash. 'Are you sickening for something?' he said.

Janice forced a smile and poured the lager. He didn't like a big head on his beer, so she had to concentrate on that. Everything had to be just so. 'I'm fine,' she said, keeping her voice quiet, so it didn't sound like she was whining. Rob hated it when she whined.

'Well, you're obviously not,' he said. 'You're going round with a face like a dug's arse, so you're not fine, are you?'

He gave her a bright, conclusive smile, then carried on eating. It wasn't fair. She looked after her teeth; he never did. But then, he never had any problems with his health. Especially not with his teeth. He hadn't been to the dentist's in years, he would say. Not since school, in fact.

They were all thieves, dentists. Sometimes, when he was at a barbecue or a party, he would prise the top off a beer bottle with his front teeth and spit it out with a big grin. Then he would tip the bottle up and down it in one, the froth gurgling over the rim and running down his chin. 'I've just got a bit of a toothache,' she said. 'It'll soon pass.'

Rob picked up his fork and twirled the pasta round on it. Bits of mushroom and grated cheese spun out across the table, but he didn't notice. He really did like pasta and, usually, it put him in a good mood for the rest of the evening if they had spaghetti bolognese, or that nice penne and seafood recipe she'd got out of the paper. He'd worked in an Italian restaurant one time, and he could tell you all the names of the different pasta shapes. Vermicelli. Fusilli. Linguine. Bucatini. Spaccatelli. He'd only been a kitchen porter, but he knew them all. 'It bloody well better,' he said, when he'd finally collected a good forkful. 'You can't go wandering around with a face like that.' He put the fork in his mouth and bit off the loose ends of spaghetti, then he took a sip of his beer. 'It's depressing,' he said.

Janice looked at her plate. She didn't feel like eating now, the pain was that bad, but she knew she would have to. He couldn't stand waste. 'I'll be fine,' she said, hoping to have done with it. Rob didn't say anything then, so she tried a mouthful of spaghetti. The sauce was hot and sharp in her mouth, but she swallowed it down anyway.

'Oh, for Christ's sake!' he said, letting his cutlery fall to the table. Janice put hers down too and waited. The thing to do, when he was angry, was to stop everything and let him say what he needed to say. He sat quietly for a moment, considering, then he took a sip of his lager and sat back. 'What's wrong with it anyway?'

'It's just a bit tender,' she said.

'Well, is it rotten?'

'I don't think so—'

'There must be something wrong with it,' he said. He stood up and walked round the table to where she was sitting. 'Let's have a look.' He took her by the chin and pushed her head back.

'Open wide,' he said.

She opened her mouth. She realised, as she did, that she had bad breath and she didn't want him to smell it. 'I don't think—'

'I can't see when your gums are flapping,' he said. He brought his face close to hers, so she could smell the beer. It was like when they had sex, on Saturday nights, that beer smell in her nose and mouth, him moving her about like a doll. 'Which one is it?' he said, twisting her head around to get a better light.

'It's—'

'Ah!' He released her suddenly and stepped back. 'Well,' he said. 'You've really let that go. Is this the first you've noticed?'

Janice didn't say anything. There was nothing to say. She'd known the tooth was bad, but she also knew that she couldn't go to a dentist. They were all private now, and even when they weren't, they still cost money. These days, she didn't have enough for the housekeeping, never mind the dentist. So it was pointless talking about it and, in the meantime, the food would be getting cold. He'd probably blame her for that, too.

'Well,' Rob said. 'You'll have to get it seen to.'

She stared at her spaghetti. 'I'm sure it will pass,' she said. 'Anyway, it's too expensive.'

That shut him up for a minute. He hated it when she talked about money. He hated it, that she was always so negative, always going on about what they couldn't afford. But then, even he knew how little they had, now that she wasn't working any more, and him being only casual. It had been all right when she was still at the hospital, but he'd made her give that up, because the early start time didn't work with his schedule. She'd liked that job, too. Playing with the kids when they first came in, then making sure the grown-ups were all right when the little ones went into theatre. Mostly, the parents didn't know how badly it would affect them, when little Angela or Tommy went under, there one moment, gone the next. It was a shock, seeing that happen – and then they had to go out and wait on the ward till some complete stranger was finished working on their child with swabs and scalpels. Some of them got pretty upset and it was Janice's role to be with them then and provide reassurance. That was a big responsibility – and she'd hated Rob when he'd told her that she had to give it up. But then, he couldn't have understood what it was like, because he'd never had a job like that, where you were dealing with people on a regular basis.

Rob was back in his chair now, drinking his beer. Janice could see that he was thinking, which wasn't a good sign. She wound some spaghetti round her fork. Maybe, if she just went on as normal, he would let it go.

'You're right,' he said, after a moment. 'It's too expensive.' He finished the beer, then set the glass on the table and gave her a pointed look. Janice got up immediately and went to the fridge for another tin. She opened it carefully, and put it down where he could reach it easily. She only had to pour the first one. After that, he poured his own. She sat down and started on another forkful of spaghetti.

'Forget that,' he said, his voice suddenly hard. Not loud, not yet, though that would come. He thought for a moment, then he got up and walked through to the hall. She could hear him rummaging around in the cupboard by the front door and she wondered what he was doing. He wasn't gone long, though, and when he came back he was carrying his toolbox. He looked at her.

'I'll fix it,' he said.

She didn't understand at first. 'Fix what?' she said. Then she did understand and before she could stop herself, she shook her head. 'No,' she said – and she knew immediately that she had made a mistake. Rob didn't say anything, though; he just opened the toolbox and took out a pair of fine pliers, the kind electricians use.

'See,' he said. 'I've got everything the dentist has, in my toolbox. It might not be as shiny, but with all that money he's raking in, he can afford to have shiny new pliers.' He looked her in the eye. 'But that's all it takes, when it comes down to it. A pair of pliers and a firm hand.'

Janice shook her head, but she didn't say anything. If she tried to disagree, he definitely wouldn't let it go. Not unless she had a practical reason why he couldn't do it. He was rummaging through the toolbox now, checking to see what else might come in useful. 'But, Rob,' she said, after a moment. She always felt strange when she said his name. It was like repeating a lie. 'It's not safe. It's not – sterile . . .'

'No problemo,' he said. 'All we need is boiling water. Like in the Westerns.'

She thought about this for a moment – and for that one moment she thought it might be a joke after all. But when he went through to the kitchen and put the kettle on, she knew he was serious. 'Please, Rob,' she said. 'Your food's getting cold.'

He didn't answer. She could hear him clattering about in the kitchen, getting something out of the press, and then the kettle boiled and he came back with a glass and a bottle of whisky that he'd won in a raffle at work. He didn't like whisky that much, so he'd hardly touched it. He put the bottle on the table, then set the glass next to it. 'Drink this,' he said.

'I'm all right,' she said. 'It's not hurting so much now.' She could hear the desperation in her voice, which meant that he could hear it too. That would only make him more determined to finish what he had started.

He ignored her. 'Anaesthetic,' he said. 'That's how they do it in the films. When they're cutting a bullet out, or something.' He took his pliers and went back to the kitchen and, for one brief instant, it crossed her mind that she could run. If she was fast, she could get out the door and be halfway downstairs before he noticed. But she didn't move. He came back with the newly sterilised pliers. 'All set,' he said. He looked at the empty glass. 'You'd better drink some of that. It'll make things a lot easier.' He set the pliers down carefully on the table, so the points didn't touch anything. 'Don't be a baby,' he said, pouring her a big glassful of the whisky. 'It'll be over before you know it.' He handed her the glass. 'Drink.'

She took the glass and raised it to her lips. The whisky smelled sweet and dark, like damp wood. She swallowed down as much as she could in one, then she swallowed again to stop from being sick. Rob stood over her until the glass was empty, then he poured another and watched till she drank that.

Then, when it was all gone, he set to work.

Afterwards, she sat in front of the TV for a long time with a towel pressed to her face while Rob got ready to go out.

He hadn't said anything when he got home, but as soon as he'd finished pulling the tooth and got himself cleaned up, he'd announced that he had to go and see Dougie down the West End. 'I'll not be long, though,' he said. He always said that – and sometimes it was true. Sometimes he would only be gone an hour. Other times he would stay out until the early morning. He liked to keep her on her toes.

He had hurt her badly this time. The tooth wouldn't come out at first, and he'd had to force it, holding her in the chair with one hand while he yanked at her jaw with the other, muttering and cursing all the time, and shouting at her to keep still so he could get a grip. At one point, the pliers had slipped, and she'd been scared that he would break one of her good teeth, but he'd kept going till it finally came loose. It took a long time, though. By the end, there was blood everywhere, on him and on her face and T-shirt, and Janice had felt sick again, from the pain and the whisky.

There was nothing on the TV. She wasn't really watching anyway, but after a while it started to depress her, so she turned it off and walked over to the window. The street below was invisible now, except for the silvery glow coming up from the shopfronts and she could see, across the roofs of the houses opposite, the twinkle and glitter of the city winding up to the Hilltown. Most of the time, it seemed grey and damp, but when it was just lights in the dark like this, it could be really beautiful. When you couldn't see the people or the cars, it was almost peaceful, almost the life she had wanted when she had first known Rob. He had been different then, and she had thought they both wanted the same things: the quiet at night, evenings at home together, relaxing music and a nice meal that she had spent hours preparing.

She remembered how he'd taken her out one Sunday afternoon when he still had the car, and they'd gone across to Fife, all the way down past St Andrews to this beach he knew near Kingsbarns. He had gone there when he was just a kid, he said, and he'd been happy in that place, which was why he wanted to share it with her. It wasn't much, and he'd been shy about it as they walked across the beach, looking out over the water. It was a cold, clear winter's afternoon, just before Christmas. There were no other people, so it was quiet too, except for the slow power of the sea, the white surge of it almost reaching their feet before streaming back in thin, glistening layers across the sand. They had walked for an hour or more, picking their way back and forth through the rock pools and the deeper soakaways that streamed down off the fields and, at the end, when she looked up, it was still day, but the moon was there, white and flaky above the water, like a chalk mark. She had been so happy that afternoon. She had loved that beach and she had loved Rob for taking her there – and it surprised her now, remembering, that it had only been three years ago.

Three years. That was all the time it had taken for him to become somebody she didn't know, and make her into somebody she didn't recognise in the mirror, somebody who had given up her job because he told her to, some-body who could sit in a chair at the kitchen table and let him prise her teeth out with electrician's pliers. Now, she was sick and in pain, and all she wanted to do was get away from him, but she knew she couldn't. She was too scared. He'd told her often enough, when he'd been drinking, that he couldn't live without her, how, if she ever left him, he didn't know what he would do. He always said that, after he'd done something bad. Tonight, probably, he'd come home with a bar of chocolate or a bottle of Babycham, and he'd sit her down at the kitchen table and tell her how sorry he was and how much he really loved her. He would ask her to forgive him, and she would, because she was scared of what would happen to her if she didn't. Then, if he wasn't too drunk, they would go to bed and he would want to do something he'd read about in *Forum*.

It was when she went back into the kitchen to get some more Anadin, that she heard the noise. It was just a rustle and, at first, she couldn't tell exactly where it was coming from. She stood at the open cupboard, counting out the pills – there were only eight of them, not enough for an overdose – and she heard the rustling noise in the corner, between the fridge and the press, or maybe in among the pipes at the back, where the dust gathered. Rob was always complaining to her about the kitchen, how she didn't clean behind things properly and that was like an open invitation for vermin to settle down and build nests and have little itty-bitty children of their own. He would do that last part in his Gary Oldman in *The Fifth Element* voice: he loved that film and he pretty well knew the script off by heart. Anyone else wanna negotiate? he would say, in his Bruce Willis voice and Dougie and the others would think he was so funny, only it wasn't funny at all, because there was always a streak of nastiness running through it. At home, when he did those voices, she always knew he was gearing up for something. Bingo! he'd say, doing Gary Oldman as the bent cop in *Leon*, whenever he caught her out, or found something she'd messed up. He'd done it so often, she got scared whenever Gary Oldman was on the telly. It didn't matter what film he was in. She got so scared, she could feel it in her chest and throat, like a scream she couldn't get out.

She took two of the Anadin, and washed them down with some water. Rob had left the whisky on the kitchen table and she thought about drinking more of it. Maybe with the pills it would make her sick enough so she'd have to go to the hospital, but she knew that was no good either. That would just be showing Rob up, and she would have to pay for it, sooner or later. She stood a moment, trying to get her head straight. She didn't feel drunk at all, just woozy and battered. If she went to bed and pretended to be asleep, maybe he wouldn't bother her when he got back. Maybe he would be too drunk for sex and he'd just get in beside her and pass out. Best would be if he got a carryout and went back to Dougie's, of course, but there wasn't much hope of that. Not unless Dougie had the money to sub him, which was unlikely. Her mind was going round in circles now and she knew she shouldn't have taken more pills, not on top of all that whisky. She thought about having a shower, but her mind rebelled at that – she wanted to have blood on her when he came in, so he wouldn't forget what he had done. She wanted to look a mess, so he wouldn't want to have sex, though she didn't suppose he'd care what she looked like, if he came back steaming. He probably wouldn't even notice.

The noise came again and this time she pinpointed it exactly. It was in the far corner, by the tumble dryer her mum had given them – and now that she looked, she could see something, though she couldn't make out what it was. Her vision was blurry, and what she could see was something vague and unfinished, like a scribble in blue ink among the wet shadows – something impossible, she thought, though it was definitely there. A misshapen clutch of blue fur, half-formed and not quite solid, like that stuff you find under the bed in some old person's house, where nobody's done any cleaning for years. That was what it looked like, for a moment; but then it moved, and that sound came again, first a rustle, then a scratching sound, like an animal trying to burrow through damp plaster. Which was exactly what it was, she saw, as she moved closer and peered into the powdery, soap-scented nook of dirty-white linoleum between the tumble dryer and the wall: an animal, though what kind of animal she couldn't say, because her eyes were so blurry and the shadows made it difficult to see.

At first, she thought it looked like a tiny, malnourished cat, only it was blue and too small even for a kitten; then, as her eyes adjusted, she saw that it was a fox, or something like a fox, with that keen, clever face a fox has in children's books. The quick brown fox jumps over the lazy dog. Only that was impossible, because foxes weren't blue and, anyway, how would a fox get into her kitchen, high up on the third floor of a tenement block in the middle of Dundee? And how could a fox be so small? Because now that she looked closely, she could see that it was small, far too small for a fox or a kitten or even a rat. It was tiny — which meant that it had to be something else, something possible. Maybe a mouse that had escaped from some kid's house and crawled up here to be safe. You could get pet mice in all different colours now: white, black, yellow and probably, for all she knew, they had blue ones too. She bent closer and stared at the thing, as it pressed against the wall, scratching desperately at the damp plaster — and now that her eyes were getting clearer, she could see that it really was a mouse. A small, long-haired, powder-blue mouse with tiny feet and a sharp, clever face, gazing up at her from the shadows. She was surprised to realise that she wasn't afraid, but the animal was. It was terrified, in fact, and desperate to get out, scared and lost and far from its own kind, its wet, black eyes gazing up at her, so shiny and wet and hopeless that she felt a sudden, desperate need to gather it up and spirit it away before Rob got home. To save it, in other words — because Rob would kill it, if he found it there. It wouldn't matter that it was blue and somebody's pet, he would kill it anyway, because he hated vermin. He would kill it without a second thought and Janice knew that she couldn't let that happen. She had to pick the thing up and get it out of there, maybe let it loose on the stairs and see if it found its own way home or, better yet, carry it out to the little drying green behind the tenements and set it down in the grass, so it could scuttle off into the dark.

She needed to save it – she didn't know why but she had to – and, really, it wasn't that big a deal. All she had to do was be confident, like her granddad had told her to be, when she was little and still living at home. Back then, the neighbourhood kids would always be coming by to tell him about a hurt thrush or a starling they had found in the woods, or out on the old farm road and, when they did, he would immediately put down what he was doing and follow them out to where the bird was, a big, calm man in his shirtsleeves, surrounded by hushed, excited boys. Then, half an hour later, he would come back, the bird still and watchful in his hand, attentive to all that was happening, but not really scared, because it sensed the gentleness in him. He'd explained to her, once, how that was all it took, when you were dealing with animals and birds. If you were calm, they were calm. If you were scared, they would be scared. All she had to do was be confident.

Only, she had no idea how to catch a living animal, and even after she'd told herself that it was just a tiny thing, alone and defenceless and probably more terrified than she was, the idea of picking it up still frightened her. Nevertheless, she forced herself to hunker down and make a cradle of her hands, willing the mouse to be still just long enough for her to scoop it up out of this dim, soap-scented corner and carry it away. She didn't know what time it was, but she knew that Rob might come back at any minute. So she had to be quick, and she had to be decisive. Decisive and confident and, most of all, calm.

She got down on one knee. The mouse had stopped moving and turned slightly and, though it wasn't looking at her any more, it knew she was there. It didn't panic, though, and it didn't try to run away as, inch by inch, she closed in. Then, suddenly, her hand darted out, of its own volition – one hand, not two, as she had originally intended – and she had the mouse in her half-closed fist, a little sack of hair and bones, not struggling, not moving at all, in fact, and utterly silent. For a moment, everything was still. She lifted her hand slightly to peer at the mouse – and it seemed at first that she had missed altogether and scooped up nothing but dust and air. Then, as she brought her half-closed fist closer, she saw its face. She couldn't tell what it was thinking, but it didn't look scared any more, it just seemed to be listening for something, far off in the distance.

It had ears that were too large for its head and its mouth looked tiny and clenched, as if someone had stitched it shut with fine black thread. Before, she had thought it would be plump and round and warm in her fist; now that she had it, she could feel how cold and insubstantial it was. That surprised her more than anything. It was nothing, really, the merest wisp of a thing that she couldn't help thinking would vanish altogether, if she tightened her grip any further – and even before she turned to go into the other room, even before she heard Rob's key in the front door, she could feel it shrinking, so that, for one brief moment, she thought she was crushing it, even though her hand was so careful, so soft. That was what she had been afraid of, when she first thought to pick it up: she hadn't been scared for herself, she had been afraid she would hurt the mouse in some way, without meaning to. She was afraid it would die, and it would be her fault. Yet now, as it sat snug in her hand, safe and hidden and warm, it was melting away, dwindling between her fingers to the merest clutch of hair and dust – and she knew that she'd have to get it out of the flat before it disappeared altogether.

She had only gone a couple of steps when she heard the key. First the key, then the door swinging open with that slight creak it had, and then – moment by moment, like some slow-motion soundtrack of everyday life – the sound of Rob taking off his coat and coming through, his face distant and slightly bleared from the drink. At first, he didn't even see her, standing there in the door frame between the living room and the kitchen, and she knew he'd had a good skinful, though it hardly seemed any time at all since he'd left. Then he made her out and stood a long moment, like someone peering through fog, and it reminded her of the parents in the waiting room, after their children had gone in to surgery, how they looked at her from so far away, unhappy and surprised, as if they couldn't quite remember who she was.

She had only gone a couple of steps and, all the time, as she stood facing her husband, trying to decide how drunk he might be, she could feel the last trace of the mouse wasting away – until, finally, in this state of suspended animation, she began to realise that she hadn't caught the mouse at all. She had missed it altogether and come up with nothing more than a fistful of dust and – what was that stuff you found in dark corners where nobody had cleaned? What was it called? Slut's hair. Yes; that was it. That was what her mother had always called it – slut's hair – and Janice remembered how much she had liked the sound of those words when she was little, before she knew what a slut was. Rob had called her that, once, when she'd let Dougie kiss her under the mistletoe – a fleeting brush of his lips on her cheek, not really a kiss at all – that first Christmas after they'd got married. Slut. He'd said it like he was happy, like he'd known it all along. 'You're just a little slut,' he'd said, and when she tried to laugh it off, he'd grabbed her by the throat and pushed her against the wall. 'What kind of idiot do you think I am?' he'd said, and he'd held her there till the tears came.

Now, he was staring at her, as if he was surprised not to be coming home to an empty house, and she could see that he was even drunker than she'd thought. At the same time, the thought came to her that, if she hadn't caught it before, the mouse had to be somewhere behind her still – out of harm's way, at least for the moment – and she listened, hoping she wouldn't hear anything, praying that the animal had sensed Rob coming in and had scuttled away to some dark place where he would never find it. Because she needed that mouse to be safe. It was her secret, and she had to keep it from harm. Nothing is more precious than a secret, her granddad had told her once, when she was little – and she had treasured that idea all through her school years, because there had been nothing else to treasure. All her life, she had made up secrets, inventing them out of thin air and keeping them, religiously – and now she had one again. It was nothing but a mouse, she knew that, a tiny blue mouse with a stitched-shut mouth and oversize ears, but it had come to her and nobody else, and Rob could never be allowed anywhere near it. Not now, not ever.

She felt woozy again, suddenly, and her jaw was throbbing. It must have been like that all the time, she realised, but she hadn't felt it until now. She looked at Rob. She had to make out that she was pleased to see him, she had to make him think she'd waited up for him all this time, so she could make him a coffee, or fetch him another drink, the moment he came in the door. Most of all, she had to pretend she didn't know he was drunk, because that would mean she was judging him, and he hated to be judged more than anything. She set her mouth in what she hoped was a smile. 'I was just going to put the kettle on,' she said, and she knew she was explaining herself already, which was bound to arouse his suspicions, because going to the kitchen wasn't something that needed explaining, even to him.

He wasn't suspicious, though, and she knew, with a bright surge of relief, that he wouldn't find the mouse. Not tonight, anyway. He was too drunk, and there was something else going on, a dark, bemused tangle of thoughts and emotions behind his eyes that she immediately recognised as something like regret. That was what he always did, after he'd hurt her badly. He would get drunk and then he'd be guilty. Sometimes he would say he was sorry and he would make promises for the future, sometimes he would just come and stand in front of her, waiting for a sign that they could put it all behind them. For as long as it lasted, that feeling would be genuine – and she hated him for it. 'Do you want coffee?' she said.

Rob nodded, but he didn't say anything. He was still thinking, still rehearsing the pretty little speech he would make when he was ready. Janice waited a moment, then she went back to the kitchen to boil the kettle, taking care not to look in the direction of the tumble dryer until she heard the television come on. Then, when she was completely sure she wouldn't be seen, she went over to the exact spot where she had knelt before, to make sure there was nothing that Rob might see, other than some tiny scratches in the plaster and a few scattered wisps of slut's hair, strangely lifelike and blue against the dirty-white linoleum.

PEACH MELBA

I have forgotten most of my life so far. This surprises me, sometimes, because I have enjoyed it so much: enjoyed it all, or most of it, enjoyed the summer days here in my tiny garden by the sea, enjoyed the oddly quiet companionship of marriage, enjoyed – quietly, yes, and with a more or less deliberate economy – the coming of winter, the taste of snow on the air when I walk to the village, and the strangely exotic tree – dark, and very still, with a hint of distance, a faint, almost imperceptible rumour of tundra about it – that the Rotary Club raises every year on the little green outside the church. Before I came here to live, I travelled a fair amount and I know that I enjoyed – I clearly remember enjoying – the journeys I made, mostly to the once melancholy cities of Eastern Europe – Prague, Bucharest, Sofia, Skopje – though occasionally to other places when someone was needed at short notice: Paris, say, or Tromsø; Buenos Aires, Santiago, Montevideo. I have spent time in most of the major cities of Europe and South America, but I remember very few details and, when I look back, what I see in my mind's eye is a street corner in Amsterdam or Budapest merging seamlessly into a broad, tree-lined avenue in Barcelona or Madrid: merging, or melding, swimming together the way faces in a dream merge into one eternalised other. The scent of melons reminds me of a summer I spent in Sliema, a sleepy Maltese harbour town where – in those days at least – beautiful young men would drive horse-traps up and down the promenade, and the fruit-seller rode his cart from street to street, pausing awhile outside my rented apartment to offer me dark, slightly overripe melons and prickly pears, like sacs of sweet blood, for that day's lunch. The smell of mingled dust and rain makes me think of an office in St Petersburg; or rather, the staircase I would climb every day to reach the office, being wary of Russian elevators and, for me, that scent is irrevocably combined, in a kind of mild synaesthesia, with the view of the Neva from that fourth-floor window, a view that has stayed with me, when all the people I knew there, and everything I did, have long ago slipped away into forgetting. I have passed through all these places, but I remember them only in fragments, only as glimpses, and I cannot fully separate one from another, no matter how distinct they ought to be. It can even happen that, from time to time, the glimpses remain unclassified, their location and time mislaid, till all that remains is a hummingbird poised at the mouth of a flower, or an early morning café with a caged bird on the counter that I think is probably Belgian, but could as easily be Greek; or some lamplit promenade where, long ago, I encountered a beautiful, dark-eyed woman who reminded me of someone I had met years before – reminded me of her so much in fact that, for a moment, I thought she was an apparition, a ghost from my own imagination made flesh and blood, and touched with the magic of a darkness that – in my imagination – she is never quite able to enter.

PEACH MELBA

According to my 1992 edition of Mrs Beeton's Book of Cookery and Household Management, *Georges Auguste Escoffier created this dish for Dame Nellie Melba. It 'consisted of ripe peaches poached in vanilla syrup and arranged in the centre of a bowl of vanilla ice cream'. Cold Melba sauce, made from sweetened raspberries, was poured over the peaches and the bowl containing the dessert was presented on a dish of crushed ice. Dame Nellie Melba was born Helen Mitchell in the Australian*

city of Melbourne, from which she took her stage name. Chambers
Biographical Dictionary *tells us that she 'appeared at Covent
Garden in 1888, and the wonderful purity of her soprano voice
won her worldwide fame'.*

It sounds foolish to say so now, but I always imagined I
would see that ghost again. Even when I was happily
married, even when I was busy with a job that made
absurd demands on my time, even in the first days of
solitude, when I realised that, of all the final states I had
imagined for myself, I had never once considered that of
widower, I thought she would reappear, not as a phantom,
not for a passing moment, but as something permanent.
A presence, a palpable being. I once dreamed that my
wife and I had a child, and it grew up to be a replica, in
every detail, of this dark-eyed Italian woman whom I had
known – if *known* is the appropriate word here – for less
than an hour, twenty-five years before. There were times
when I would wake in the dark, next to my quiet wife,
who always slept so soundly, childlike in her own dream
place, her hair smelling of bread and rain, a half-smile
playing across her lips – there were times when I woke in
the dark and imagined I had committed some terrible
crime, a beautiful, perfect crime that had gone undetected
for a lifetime, but must now be confessed and, if possible,
forgiven. I would lie there for long minutes in a state of
panic, trying to remember what I had done – and it was
this, the fact that I could not remember, that troubled
me, far more than the notion of having done something
terrible. How could I be forgiven, if I could not remember
my sin? How could I ever repent, if I imagined myself
blameless?

Yet I *was* blameless – and in my waking hours I knew
that I was. If I thought about it, if I considered the facts,
I could say: I met her by accident, in the ice-cream parlour
she ran with her husband and his mother; I met her by

chance, because her children, Vincent and Angela, were at school with me, and if the fault belonged to anyone, it was theirs. Vincent was the classroom heart-throb, a confident, slightly cruel boy with Hollywood–Italian, matinee idol looks in the making, and I admired him desperately. He was clever, but never a show-off; he had a wonderful disdain for priests and teachers, which he managed to communicate without ever being openly impolite; he was beautifully arrogant, with that air of knowing something I could only guess at: one of the keepers of the important secrets that only such a boy could know, a reader of faces, a nightwalker, a collector of exquisite private moments. Or so it seemed. His sister was a year older, but she and Vincent were very close, almost unnaturally so, in spite of an age difference that, at thirteen, was more significant than it would ever be again. He was the only boy she tolerated; the rest she looked down upon with the contempt of a girl already on her way to developing breasts and a pair of wide, Sophia Loren eyes, and who was therefore an object of bedazzled curiosity for every boy she met – and for the men too, perhaps. Like Vincent, she knew things; like Vincent, she saw through everyone – and this was their special secret, this private knowingness that they had agreed, at some point in their young lives, not to turn upon one another. At home, they spoke Italian with their grandmother; in that mostly poor town, they had books of their own that were not borrowed from the school library, or a sympathetic teacher. Their father gave them outrageous sums of pocket money and took them in his car to places we could not have visited on the bus. One year they went 'home' to Italy, to see relatives, and they came back brown as berries, with the knowing half-smiles of children who have visited the outside world, and had secrets they could have told, had they so wished.

Most of all, they lived in the House of Ice Cream. That was the name of their father's ice-cream parlour, a play, as

I now know, on the family name. It was a beautiful name: Della Casa, perfectly Italian somehow, and I thought, when I first learned what it meant, how foolish their father had been to squander that music, just for the sake of wordplay. But then, that was part of the Della Casa charm, that ability to squander. The sweets they made – peach Melba, Neapolitan ice, knickerbocker glory, banana splits – were luxurious and gaudy confections that, in those years just after rationing, seemed extraordinary self-indulgences, and the only way to mark a special occasion, for adults and children alike. Yet it wasn't the ice creams that made for glamour, so much as the fact that these children virtually lived in the shop, helping out, or minding the till, wandering back into the kitchens where other children were never allowed, sitting at their own table with cups of coffee and slivers of thin, fawn-coloured toast that, like the house speciality, was also named for the great diva, talking quietly to one another in their own secret talk, or calling out in Italian to the women in the back of the shop, to the grandmother, who was only rarely seen, and to the mother, who was more or less invisible. No wonder I adored them, no wonder I knelt down at Mass and, with a lingering sense of committing some terrible blasphemy, prayed, after my own fashion, for them to accept me, to take me in, to make me a creature of their world, however lowly, and for however short a time.

The soul is present at the beginning, like mind, or grammar, but it takes a lifetime to emerge fully into its true being, like those desert plants that flower only once, every hundred years or so. Everyone is headed towards something, everyone is travelling towards a specific end, making tracks for the inevitable: not death, or not just death, but something else, something equally mysterious. For me, it is a memory, a single, perfectly defined moment for which all the other moments have been surrendered, and to that extent it is a matter of choice. A choice made in the darkest

shadows of the psyche, perhaps, but a choice, nevertheless. We are,
as we grow older, the products of the choices we make, both
conscious and unconscious, and the only wisdom we can ever
attain is the wisdom to know how the process works, at the most
hidden level. Our conscious and our secret choices sometimes
contradict one another, that is only to be expected. There are
choices we learn to make, and there is the matter of the soul,
which operates beyond convention or common sense. The best
fortune a man can have is to choose with his soul, rather than
with his heart or his head because, then, there is always a secret,
there is always a place in his marrow that remains intact, sacred
and untouchable, a noli me tangere *place, like that shadowy*
place in the garden where Mary encountered Jesus, and didn't
even know who he was.

I was fairly shameless in my pursuit of the Della Casas
– which seems odd, looking back, after a life in which
friends mattered little to me, a life in which my colleagues,
my neighbours, even most of my family are barely remembered. Perhaps it has to do with what happened that
summer. I am not one to believe in simple cause and
effect, especially of the psychological variety, but the fact
is that I have never had, nor have I ever missed having,
any particular or special friends. My closest friend was
probably my wife, but even she was something of a mystery
to me – as I was, no doubt, to her. I do not mean by this
that she was in any way perplexing; far from it. The truth
is, I cultivated the mystery between us: I made it happen,
with all kinds of slight yet deliberate ruses and tricks. I
was quiet. I was unforthcoming. I was also away much
of the time and, when I was home, I moved silently around
the house as if I were a ghost, or a servant, taking care of
things, making sure she had everything she might need,
leaving little gifts where she could find them, knick-knacks
and curiosities from my travels, lavishly wrapped boxes of
the chocolates I knew she liked best, rare or at least

interesting examples of the netsuke she liked to collect, tiny mice nestling in the gnawed interiors of tiny pumpkins, improbable sea creatures, smiling frogs, ivory rats. All through our marriage, even during the years when I was so often away from home, I took an interest in everything she did, from the netsuke to the garden she cultivated so assiduously in my absence. No one could have said that we were unhappy: we were companions, a neat fit, and we could say our marriage was good, beyond question. It was only when she died, and I buried her just as quietly as we had lived, with the minimum of fuss and bother, that I realised that she, having come as close to me as anyone had ever come, was really not that close to me at all. It was just that we were both close to the same things, the same house, the same way of life.

So why I should have wanted so much to be friends with the Della Casas is something of a mystery to me now. I suppose, back then, I imagined, as children do, that friends were a necessity in life, like a bicycle, or money; I suppose I thought that a boy without friends was somehow inadequate. Perhaps I was piqued by their initial lack of interest, their obvious indifference that, because they were so much better than me, bore no trace of malice or venom. I suspect nothing is as beguiling to a child as disdain – and Vincent Della Casa was a child prodigy in that art. In fact, it was only through his sister, the impossibly beautiful, improbably sophisticated Angela, that I ever got close enough to be invited to go to the carnival with them at all. Of course, in spite of her good offices, that carnival day didn't turn out the way I had planned it – and there is a distinct possibility that they never meant it to end in anything other than tears. Yet, even now, I like to think she was sincere in her efforts on my behalf. I like to think that someone so beautiful harboured some kindly impulse behind that cool exterior. It's one of the temptations of beauty, I suppose. We want beauty to be truth, and truth beauty, and it feels like a betrayal – even to us, the unlovely – when it is not.

I had tried for months to befriend Vincent, to no avail. Then, all of a sudden, everything changed. It was late in the holidays – the Thursday before the carnival, as I recall. I was standing by myself at the back wall of the play park, at the single vantage point that allowed me to see into the neighbouring garden, where the Covington sisters lived. The Covington sisters, Martha and Mary, loved wild-life, and they had arranged their garden to draw in birds I had never seen anywhere else, tree-creepers and nuthatches, long-tailed tits, odd, unidentified migrants that, having strayed off their normal course, had been lured into Martha and Mary's garden of earthly delights. You could see birds there all year round, but in summer, there were vagrants and mysteries to be witnessed, and the air overhead was busy with swallows, criss-crossing back and forth in pursuit of flies. The Covington women were spinsters and they had lived together in that house since the dawn of time. Nobody ever spoke to them; even the baker and the butcher's boy exchanged their goods for the correct sums of money, counted out in advance and handed over on the doorstep, without ever speaking a word. Sometimes, however, if I was patient, I could hear one or other of them speak in a quiet sing-song, and I was enchanted by the sound, enchanted by the way they were slowly changing, one day at a time, into the things they most loved.

It was Angela who found me there. She appeared at my shoulder, as if from nowhere, and gave me a curious look. 'What are you doing?' she asked.

I didn't know what to say. I waved my hand vaguely in the direction of the Covingtons' garden, and hoped that would be sufficient explanation.

Angela smiled. 'Birdwatching,' she said.

I nodded. Someone else laughed, somewhere behind

me, and I turned. I hadn't known Vincent was there too, watching from about ten feet away, and I felt suddenly unhappy, as if they had caught me out in some way, doing something foolish or private.

'You like birds,' Angela continued. She smiled patiently, as if addressing a child.

'Yes,' I said. 'They're all right.'

Vincent came closer. 'There's a carnival, this Saturday,' he said.

I nodded. 'Yes,' I said. 'I know.' The fair came to town every summer but, that year, the council had decided it would be a carnival. To us, it had the sound of new times, of glamour and money and the end of the post-war austerity that had designated everything from sausages to kisses, if not scarce, then unjustified indulgences. Times had been hard and now they were going to be better. If only the powers-that-be had thought of it before, all they needed to keep us happy and malleable was a man on stilts and a parade along the high street, with ponies and ballerinas, balloons and floats, children waving flags and cheering, grown-ups in their church clothes eating candy floss. By today's standards, it was nothing special – a parade, a fair on the waste ground near the old telephone exchange, makeshift stalls selling hot dogs and freshly baked cakes – but for us it was an event.

'Are you going?' Vincent asked.

I wanted to seem nonchalant. I knew how unattractive eagerness seems to people like the Della Casas. 'Of course,' I said. 'The whole town will be there.'

Vincent laughed at my quaint expression and gave Angela a meaningful look. 'That's right,' he said, to her only. 'The whole town. Everybody except our mother.'

Angela looked annoyed and I knew that – for that one moment – I had been given the opportunity to see through the gorgeous surface of their lives. The trouble was, I didn't know what I was supposed to discover. I had never seen their mother. As far as I know, nobody saw her very much. What people said back then was that she liked to keep herself to herself. 'I think,' Angela said, finally, 'what my moron brother is trying to say is, would you like to come to the carnival with us?'

I couldn't believe it, of course. Go to the carnival – with them? Next, they would be suggesting we all meet up at the House of Ice Cream for a vanilla sundae before the carnival began.

'Well?' Vincent was watching me with some amusement. I suppose I looked as surprised as I felt. 'You could come round to the shop. Our mother could make us some coffee before we go.' He peered at me, as if he were looking at some alien life form. 'You do drink coffee, don't you?'

I nodded. I had never drunk coffee in my life.

Angela nodded back. 'That settles it, then,' she said. 'We'll see you at our place on Saturday at one o'clock.'

Vincent studied me a moment longer, then turned and began walking away. 'Don't be late,' he called back, without turning around. 'Or we'll go without you.'

If I said, now, that I couldn't wait for Saturday, I would be guilty of a half-truth. The fact is, I was almost as afraid of that blessed day as I was looking forward to it. I spent the whole of Friday wondering what I would say to these golden children, what I would do, how much money I could get out of my parents so I wouldn't look foolish, whether I should offer to pay for my coffee, and a hundred other minor details of form and etiquette. Oddly enough, it was the first and the last time such questions ever occurred to me, and I suppose I have the Della Casas to thank for that. With the benefit of hindsight, I can see that the day we had planned to spend together would have been a disaster of the kind that makes a person self-conscious for years, if not for a lifetime. As it happened, however, I need not have worried. I didn't have a date with Vincent and Angela, I didn't go to the carnival and, betrayed, ashamed, and thereby liberated from all further concerns with the social niceties, I didn't have to be anything other than the awkward and solitary child I had always been. I didn't even get to taste coffee until much, much later.

Somewhere, in some virtual library, there is a book to which my life is one long commentary. Not, I suspect, Moby-Dick *or* Bleak House, *or even* How to Make Friends and Influence People. *Maybe something more like* Household Management, *by Mrs Beeton, all recipes and tips on etiquette, the cure for croup or how to get dried bloodstains out of suede. What that book should contain is a matter of some importance to me: no scriptures – that goes without saying – but maybe the odd, more or less dubious, more or less true old wives' tale, some fragments of history and geography, a few tables and logarithms, perhaps, and – of this I feel quite certain – several pages of nothing but lists. There will be some foxing, naturally, and possibly a dark, camel-shaped ink stain on the spine, but what matters is that, somewhere in a margin, or in a tiny, almost illegible footnote, all of my real and imaginary lovers are mentioned by name.*

When I arrived at what Vincent had called 'the shop', nobody was there. I had never seen the House of Ice Cream empty before, and it was eerie, standing in that sunlit space, all the booths empty along the wall, the tables by the window deserted, nobody hurrying about taking orders, nobody behind the counter, watching the till. I didn't know what to do, finding it so still and, for a moment, I felt like an intruder, a burglar maybe – an ice-cream thief – or maybe a ghost. Then a tall, dark, astonishingly beautiful woman appeared from the kitchen beyond the counter, wiping her hands on a crisp white tea towel, wandering through to the front of the shop with the air of someone who knows, and is glad, that she is alone. I'm not sure that she saw me at first, or if she did, she seemed not to be convinced I was really there, and it made me feel more like a ghost than ever. She waited a long moment, staring at me, a puzzled look on her face, as if she had found some exotic animal in her ice-cream parlour, and wasn't quite sure how to handle it. Then she smiled.

'Hello,' she said. 'Can I help you?' She had a strong accent, but I understood her. It was just that I didn't know, for a minute, what to say. Her smile faded. 'Are you OK?' she asked. 'You look—'

'I'm fine,' I said. 'It's just . . .' Suddenly I was aware that I was staring at her. She was, I realised, Vincent and Angela's mother, the famously reclusive Mrs Della Casa, who always stayed in the back rooms and never spoke to anybody, but let her husband and the old woman look after the customers while she, like the great chef, Escoffier, concocted extraordinary confections in the kitchen. 'I'm Henry,' I said. 'I'm a friend of Vincent's.' It felt like a lie, saying it and, though it wasn't exactly untrue, I could see that she didn't quite believe me. 'I was supposed to meet him here. We're going to the carnival,' I added, having come to the realisation, at that very moment, that we were not.

'I'm sorry,' Mrs Della Casa said, 'but Vincent isn't here. I thought he had already gone . . .' She gave me a weak smile to hide a concern that had more to do with my presence than with her children's bad manners. 'They're not here,' she added, a little shamefaced, as if she thought I suspected her of lying.

I looked around the empty shop. 'No,' I said. 'I suppose I made a mistake—'

'No.' She seemed offended by the idea, as if she had just realised that she herself had been guilty of some terrible inhospitality. 'I'm sure it's not your fault.' She shifted awkwardly from one foot to another. She was a very beautiful woman, perhaps the most beautiful I have ever seen, and at that moment, awkward, embarrassed, unsure of what to do next, she looked more beautiful to me than seemed possible for any merely human creature.

'I'd better get off, then,' I said.

I had tried to keep the reluctance out of my voice, but she sensed it anyhow and, besides, her sense of propriety was roused. 'No,' she said. 'You should wait.' She glanced briefly at the back of the shop, as if she were afraid someone was listening, then she continued. 'Listen,' she said. 'I'm going to make you a peach Melba. Have you ever had a *real* peach Melba?'

I shook my head. I wanted to say that I would have preferred a coffee, but I didn't. 'It's all right,' I said lamely. I was remembering my mother's favourite advice to me, offered in every possible situation, an ugly phrase that every child loathes. *Don't be a bother.* And the truth was, I didn't want to be a bother. I wanted to sneak home with my tail between my legs, and curse this woman's children for the devils they were.

But Mrs Della Casa had different ideas. She had allowed herself to be offended by some idea that had crossed her mind and was off again, before I could say anything. 'I don't mean peach Melba the way some people make it,' she said. 'I mean proper, the way we make it here at the House of Ice Cream.' The way she said it, with just a hint of absurd exaggeration, made me realise she had been against the idea of the anglicised sign that hung outside the shop. She was Italian, and she saw no reason to be anything else, I suppose. She smiled at me, but there was a hint of pride in her face. 'The way *I* make it,' she said. 'The best peach Melba ever.'

I nodded. I really hadn't wanted to be a bother, but I couldn't resist the offer and, besides, it seemed to me, at that moment, that she wanted to make this exotic dessert even more than I wanted to stay and eat it. 'I don't want to be any trouble,' I let out weakly.

Mrs Della Casa was serious again, all of a sudden. 'No trouble,' she said. 'You sit down. Over there, by the window. I'll be back in fifteen minutes.'

So I sat. Part of me expected Vincent and Angela to turn up after all, but the idea gave me no pleasure. Suddenly, it was a quiet delight to be there, in that empty ice-cream parlour, while everyone else was a few streets away, out in the glare of the sun, unblessed by these soft shadows, by the gold of the muted light behind the counter and the quiet that ruled while, somewhere in the kitchen, Mrs Della Casa made me a peach Melba the old-fashioned way, with fresh peaches and crushed ice, and her own special raspberry sauce that, when the dish arrived, seemed impossibly red, impossibly *crimson*. It took less time to create than I had expected, but it was, as she had predicted, a kind of miracle, a magical thing that, sitting there on the table before me, seemed beyond time, beyond the flow of ordinary events and worries, beyond everything but love and art.

'Enjoy!' Mrs Della Casa said, as she presented me with this masterpiece – then she started away, still half-smiling, pleased, it seemed, to have done this one thing for a boy she had assumed must be sad, or lonely, or upset. I wanted to detain her, then; I wanted her to stay with me, so I could let her see that I was none of those things – that I was, in fact, quite inanely happy. 'I'm just going to the kitchen,' she said, as she passed the counter. 'I'll let you enjoy it by yourself, and when you're finished, you can tell me how you liked it.' And with that, she disappeared, out of the column of gold sunlight where she had been standing, and into the darkness beyond.

I sometimes ask myself what happened to the boy I am remembering now. Was he me? Am I him? I can imagine him disappearing a long time ago, leaving a space that anything could have filled – a potted plant, a cat, a photograph album – a boy with my face

*and hands who woke one morning and left the house early,
dressed in the usual clothes, with a satchel on his back, a boy who
seemed like any other, going about the usual work of a Wednesday
morning. He got up, splashed cold water on his face, put some
books and pencils into that bag and left the house, but he never
appeared in school, not that morning, and not on any of the mornings
that followed, a boy with my name and blood cells and hair, dressed
in my waterproof jacket and gloves, walking away in the morning
rain, his absence at morning assembly green as the scent of thuja,
his Latin primer still buried amongst the slut's hair and apple cores
in the desk he left vacant, four places from the front of the class,
between Laura Costello and Tom Morgan, children he had known
all his life who only noticed him when he was gone, and only
noticed then to wonder, for a few days, or a week at most, whether
there was more to the story than whatever explanation they were
offered for his sudden disappearance.*

A short time later, Mrs Della Casa returned to the front
of the shop. She was still smiling and I knew I wasn't
being a bother to her, that she wasn't hurrying me to
leave, but she did have something on her mind and I
couldn't help thinking, even then, that her smile was just
a little too elaborate. Not forced, exactly, just too deliberate,
too kindly. She stood a moment at the till, thinking about
something, perhaps working out what she wanted to say.
'Are you OK?' she asked.

I nodded. I wondered if she knew how beautiful she
seemed to me, at that moment, if she knew that my heart
was fluttering in my throat.

'The peach Melba,' she said, serious again. 'It's good?'

I wanted to say it was perfect, that it was a miracle in
a glass bowl, an impossible event in a world where peaches
came from tins and ice cream tasted like wax – but I
couldn't say a word. I nodded again.

'Listen,' she said. 'I don't think Vincent will be here for
a while.'

I shook my head. I knew by now that I had been stood up. Vincent was at the carnival, and so was Angela. They were probably laughing at that very moment about the trick they had played on me. Or, more likely, they had forgotten me altogether, and the truth was, I didn't care.

'But I have to go out somewhere,' Mrs Della Casa continued, looking worried. 'I have to go out for some minutes, no more.' She gave me an uncertain look, as if she were trying to do some piece of complicated arithmetic in her head and, because she had not come up with a convincing answer, needed to check it with me.

'I can stay here,' I said. I wasn't sure about this, about whether this was what she wanted, or whether I could do it, but I didn't really have a choice.

'Can you?' She looked relieved. 'I won't be gone for long.'

I nodded, sure of myself suddenly. 'Absolutely,' I said. 'I'll stay here and keep an eye on things. Take as long as you like.'

She smiled again at this, though there was a darkness in her face still and I knew the errand she had to run was something she would rather have avoided. 'You're a good boy,' she said. 'I don't know why Vincent isn't here.'

I shook my head. I knew why, but I didn't really care now. 'It's fine,' I said. 'It was probably just a misunderstanding.'

Neither of us was convinced. Mrs Della Casa stood a moment longer, watching me, curious, a little puzzled. What was I doing in her ice-cream store on that particular Saturday afternoon, when the whole town was elsewhere? Why was I missing the carnival? Looking back, I see now that it was then – at that very moment when Mrs Della Casa looked at me with that question in her eyes – that my fondness for solitary weekend afternoons was born. It had never occurred to me before, but I was one of those souls who prefer to be somewhere else when the carnival

66

is passing along the high street, just as it had never occurred to me that unrequited love could be so precise and deliberate a thing, a choice that I had just that moment made, and would continue to make all my life, a private matter that had almost nothing to do with the object of that love.

Now, the two are moulded into one: solitude, quiet, the unregistered joy of sitting at a café window, gazing out at an empty street, the delicious sense of balance that comes of putting down a book and crossing an empty room to look out at the gardens, empty and still in the middle of the afternoon, when my neighbours are out at football games or supermarkets. A cat sits on the wall, a blackbird pauses on the lawn to look up, a darker shadow forms among the shadows in the holly tree, not a presence but an event, the world happening in its own time and space, outside the mind, unpeopled, witnessed by nobody – *by nobody*, really. Even if I am standing there, looking out, listening, it is the past I am seeing, the past I am hearing. I never catch up; I am never fully there. I am a millisecond behind the moment – and part of me is further back still, further away, sitting in an empty café, watching a woman turn away, hearing her say something, I'm not sure what, then seeing her pass through the double doors and out, in her gold cotton summer dress and her miraculously white apron, out into the street, out into the sunlight, out into—

Eternity. Which is as much as to say, into the moment when she stops just beyond the kerb, remembers she is still wearing her apron, and pauses a second – a second, no more – to take it off. It's only the briefest of pauses, only the slenderest moment of inattention but, in that second, on a day when there had been no traffic for as long as I had been sitting in the House of Ice Cream, a van came speeding along the road – a little blue van, like the one the butcher used for deliveries – and struck her, full force, throwing her up into the air and away, out of my line of vision. For a moment, it seemed unreal, like a trick she or someone was playing on me, or maybe a rehearsal for something that wasn't decided yet. Then I heard the noise of the brakes, as the van screeched to a halt, and somebody screamed. I jumped up and ran to the door – and all of a sudden, as if they had all been waiting for something to happen, there were people everywhere: a man bending over the fallen woman, another man standing by the door of the van, where the driver sat, staring at what he had done, in total shock. It wasn't the butcher, I saw. It was someone I had never seen before. I'm not sure what I would have done, or what I wanted to do. Perhaps I would have run to where Mrs Della Casa lay, so still, so obviously dead, but someone else had come, also from nowhere, and he was holding on to me, holding my shoulders, not very forcefully, but enough so I could give in and not move, so I could only stand and stare as, for one long minute, everything stopped and a hole appeared in the universe I had known till then, a hole that was tiny and white and lit by the sun, a hole that, to any other eye, looked like a clean, but slightly creased apron, lying on the tarmac, where Veronica Della Casa had dropped it.

Why does one moment have so much power? Nothing that seems significant, no well-remembered, landmarked victory or loss makes the soul what it is; rather, it is the passing moment, the thing half-seen, that sets the pattern – the key of a life, you could almost say – the home key, yes, from which the piece might stray for a while, but to which it must always return. I have forgotten most of my life so far. People told me, when I was young, that I would remember more when I was older and I trust that I will, I trust that, as this quiet time in my final home lengthens and deepens, I will stop remembering every detail of the book I just read, or the conversation I had at the butcher's yesterday, and my mind – stiller now, quieter – will begin to piece together the corpus of my life, moment by moment, year by year, as an

*archaeologist puts together a man from a scatter of bones he has
found in a midden. If it is true, I look forward to that. I look
forward to the day when I pass a girl on the library steps and,
because patchouli is back in fashion, because her hair has been
brushed back in a certain way, because she is light of foot and
slender and open in a way that nobody has seemed to me in
years, I will remember myself as a young man, and so solve the
mystery of who it was lived in my place, breathing and eating
and making love through all those lost years. I look forward to
the day when I remember my wife as she was when we met,
and not the golden, but slightly distant creature she became later.
I look forward to having memories that I can see and smell: brief,
but intense madeleine moments when everything comes back to
me in gorgeous detail. I rather suspect, however, that I will not
remember anything clearly again, that I will continue to live in
this limbo of unclassified sensations and mental snapshots till
that promised moment when, at the very last, everything flashes
before my eyes once more, a whole history unfolding and coming
to life behind my eyes in milliseconds, like those Japanese paper
toys that, the moment they are immersed in water, blossom into
extraordinary and elaborate flowers: peonies, chrysanthemums,
irises, lilies. Perhaps then the moment when Mrs Della Casa
died will be just one of many moments, one flower in a bowl of
brilliantly coloured flowers, unfolding and spreading in my memory,
a petal at a time.*

On Saturday afternoons, I make myself a peach Melba. I
make it the way Mrs Della Casa made it, or I like to think
I do. It never quite tastes the way it ought, but then I
could hardly expect a miracle of such proportions. These
days, I could use better ingredients – freshly picked peaches,
fuzzed with warmth and static; organic ice cream; vanilla
pods from the Fairtrade store – but I stick to the ingredients she was obliged to use, because what I am searching
for is not a perfect peach Melba, not a copy of Escoffier's
original recipe, but the repetition of a moment. When

I am done, I sit down at the table by the window and think about the high street, about the people elsewhere, crossing roads, shopping, meeting friends, stopping to talk for a moment, then moving on. I have to admit that I feel a certain quiet, slightly detached affection for them all: men, women, children; shop assistants, cooks, hospital porters; police superintendents, typists, spies. I think of the House of Ice Cream – it calls itself a bistro now, and the Della Casas are long gone – as it was once upon a time, and how it might have been, had it survived. This is a scientific experiment, an attempt to fix a soul in place, like a butterfly on a pin, to see it entire and motionless for a moment. I think of the sun on a plate-glass window and a blue van passing along a street, then I try to slow it all down, to see what really happened, to isolate the moment when I became someone other than I had been, someone other than the person I had been destined to be. It's the only moment of my life that I remember, and even then I cannot quite see it entire. Here, from where I am sitting, I can see the garden, where a wave of forget-me-nots flows from under the shade of a currant bush and fades into the gravel path. I can look up and watch the swallows flicker out from the brickwork on James and John Street, watch them scouting the warm air above the hedges, a constant play of shadows and light, but even as it happens it is receding into the past – it is all going and, when I try to grasp it, there is no now, no present moment, no fixed self to slip into and *be*, once and for all. I would like to say that peach Melba – the taste of the ice cream, or the way the raspberry bleeds into the ice and stains it a dark crimson – I would like to say that *something* brings it all back to me, but I cannot. What I taste is ice cream and peaches, what I see is crimson, what I hear is the twittering of the swallows overhead and, after all these years, I still cannot tell where my self leaves off and the world begins, as everything – self and world, soul and matter

– falls away into nothingness, beautifully, elegantly, and as it must, leaving me stunned and bereft, and alone in my house, lost, or perhaps merely suspended, in the lingering and slightly overblown perfection of peach Melba.

SUNBURN

Every year, on the first really hot day of summer, I get sunburn. I go out into the garden, or I'm sitting on a beach, and I take off my shirt, just for a moment, to cool off, or to feel the year's first warmth on my back and shoulders. All the time, I am planning to cover up after fifteen minutes, or at most, half an hour; all the time, I know exactly where things are headed. I am fair-haired and light-skinned and I burn easily. I should be using a high-factor sunscreen; better still, I should keep my shirt on my back, where it belongs, because I know, from years of experience, that as soon as I feel the heat beating down on my neck and arms, I fall asleep. I drift away, I dream, the dreams are complicated and utterly compelling, tiny myths unfolding in my head. Then I sleep for an hour, or an afternoon and, by the time I realise what has happened, my back is red and my arms are already tingling. When I pull my shirt on, an exquisite shiver runs across my skin, part pleasure, part pain, fleeting and dark, like the wind on a field of ripening corn. An hour later, I am raw.

The sad thing is, I know why this happens, but I keep on doing it. Whenever I hear someone say that self-knowledge is the key to a happy life, I have to laugh. It's not that I'm against self-knowledge, as such; but, for me, it's just a hobby, like every other form of knowledge. Whatever we need to do, we do it, again and again, once the pattern is established. We can go to therapists, we can read self-help books, but we either continue doing what we have done all along, or we become something less than we were. Like Cindy, for example. Cindy has read every self-improving book under the sun and, as a result, she spends most of her life as a shadow of her real and inevitably mysterious self, doing what she thinks she ought to be doing, practising reiki and emotional intelligence, eating food from a book and asking for help from her peers when she feels a little fragile. She's like a well-tended suburban garden: a little too tidy, a little too well managed. Meanwhile, I go about my business, doing what I have to do and, beyond that, as little as possible. Every year, on the first really hot day of summer, I get sunburn. Some years I burn quite badly; others, only a little. It doesn't matter, though; it has to happen. It's how I remember the story that my body is telling, a story that, for much of the time, is really rather pleasant, in spite of how things sometimes appear.

This story begins in the summer of my fourteenth year. From the off, I was one of those reclusive, moody children who lie awake at night and wish they had a talent of some kind, cryptography, say, or music. At some point in the not too distant future, I thought, I would learn something that would mark me out from my peers. I would speak six languages, or I would be the one person in the entire world who could tell the wealth of some ancient civilisation from the random contents of an earthenware jar, or some arcane system of knot-work and braiding. At school, I would sit at my desk and think about the future, which was coming any day now. Meanwhile, I was alone. I didn't talk to anyone, not even to my parents – especially not to my parents – and I didn't know anyone because, like any teenage philosopher, I didn't believe it was possible to know anyone. Not, you know, *really know*. I was more or less contented with this state of affairs, or I would have been, if other people had just left me to it, but the worst thing about being almost fourteen is that people expect you to have friends, and if you don't, they worry. At fifty, say, a man can be the quiet, studious type, something of a night owl, fonder of his books, or his cat, or a good single malt than he is of company. Like my father, for example. So why was it that he, of all people, kept trying to get me to *do something*? Why did he think it was so unhealthy that I preferred not to go out and meet kids my own age, when his idea of human contact was listening to the radio? To be fifty and have no friends is a sign of thoughtfulness; to be in the same condition at fourteen is a sign of failure, if not now, then soon. If I could, I would go back and tell that almost fourteen-year-old that it was all nonsense, all that talk about going out and meeting people, and I would tell him to think less about the future and take more notice of what's passing him by, because I am rather fond of that boy, now that I no longer have to be him.

I never think about the future now. A time comes when the only meaningful work is to forget about the future altogether and return to the one thing that's always there: the present, the incalculable. A time comes when the present is all there is, and it goes on happening, as opposed to melting away, or fading into the past. The past remains, of course, as an idea; but the future is nothing at all. It's not even the source of tomorrow's, or next year's, fleeting present, the way it once seemed. A time even comes when things forget their names, when the figure you know from an old painting is crossing a street in the everyday world, an angel from a Duccio Nativity, or one of the lesser apostles in a fresco that some fifteenth-century master left to a bemused posterity. The time comes when nothing is other than it seems, when there is nothing to calculate, nothing to figure out, nothing to measure yourself against. If I could go back, I would tell that almost fourteen-year-old boy this, and a good deal more besides, though it would be ridiculous of me to expect him to listen.

The past remains, and it does no harm to visit from

time to time. Mostly, it isn't what it seems, almost all of it shifts about as we try to navigate our memories, but there are places that stay constant, whole hours at a time that never fade or alter. Like that day, when I found myself alone at home on a beautifully hot afternoon and rushed outside to sunbathe, a book in one hand, a stolen gin and tonic in the other. I didn't much like alcohol, but I felt it was my duty to drink whenever my parents went out for the day, announcing as they left that they wouldn't be back till after midnight, so I should help myself to food from the fridge, and not stay up too late because I had school in the morning, or music, or whatever else I was doing to improve myself. Even at that age I ought to have known that alcohol and hot days didn't go together; my dad had got sunstroke once from sitting in the garden all day drinking beer, and my mother was always telling him to cover up because, like me, he had pale colouring. It always felt like a failing, that pale colouring. Not an accident of nature, but something that we, the two men of the Williamson household, had not quite managed to get right.

I have no memory of falling asleep, or of how much gin I drank before I did, but I do remember our neighbour, Angela Mathers, leaning over me suddenly, her hand on my back, her voice arriving from the perfect distance of sleep. 'Hey,' she was saying. 'Wake up. You're going to fry here.' She touched me again, and I started up, electrified. She pursed her lips. 'Whoops,' she said, 'looks like you already did.' She straightened up. 'Where's Caron?' she said. 'Where's David?'

'They're out,' I said. I looked at her. At that moment the heat in my back and arms wasn't that bad, just a pleasant hum, really. The difficult fact to take in was Angela Mathers, in a short lemon-coloured summer dress standing over me with a half-worried, half-amused look on her face. 'Gone away for the day,' I added, to keep the conversation going. I didn't want her to abandon me.

'Well, I'll have to see what I can find to fix you up,' she said. 'You come indoors to the shade and I'll see what there is in the medicine chest.'

I was a little worried by this. I didn't think we had a medicine chest, as such. Still, I rose slowly, the heat in my back suddenly stinging, as my skin crinkled and buzzed, and I followed her into the house.

I had been in love with Angela Mathers for three years, ever since I'd seen her walking to work one morning in a dark-blue winter coat and navy gloves. She worked at a place that people referred to mysteriously, with a hint of knowing secrecy, as the vet lab. I had no idea what they did there, and I suspect nobody else did either, but I liked to picture her up there, in the low, thirties-style buildings that stood at the edge of the woods, conducting tests, or making long, complicated calls to scientists and technicians in Denmark or Manitoba, her soft voice fusing in the telephone lines with snowfalls and birdsong and the wind over the North Sea. Inside the vet lab, it was always evening and, when Angela Mathers emerged, at the end of a long, important day, she was touched with the shadows of elsewhere, even as she walked home in the sunshine of late afternoon. She had perfectly blue eyes that couldn't be compared to anything else I knew, and she wore her dark, not quite black hair in a tight bob, which made her look confident and deserving.

Inside I sat down in the dining room, while Mrs Mathers disappeared in search of medicaments. I had no idea what she intended; but the possibilities suddenly appeared terrifying and miraculous at the same time. I remembered her cool fingertips on my shoulder, and I thought the only thing that could possibly cure me of my ills was that coolness, that smoothness, stroking the hurt away. I felt a little dizzy. My mouth was parched. I thought of going into the kitchen for a glass of water, but I didn't want to move.

Finally she reappeared, all reassuring smiles, like a television nurse.

'Just the ticket,' she said, producing a large blue tube that I had never seen before. She unscrewed the lid. 'Now this may smart a little,' she said. 'Just you sit still.' She pulled a chair up next to mine and studied my left shoulder. 'OK, you'll live,' she said brightly. 'Here we go.' With that she set to work, and the room vanished around me, and then *I* vanished and all that remained was the cool lotion, the light pressure of her hands and a voice that I could barely follow, guiding me into the darkness.

I imagine some time passed then. I have no memory of that but, sadly, time never stops. She talked, asking me questions, drawing me out of myself, and I did my best to sound normal and grown up and casual in my replies. We talked about school, and books, and she asked if I had a girlfriend.

'No,' I said. 'There's a vacancy there.' I had no idea where this came from. Maybe the last of the gin.

She laughed. 'Well,' she said. 'If I wasn't already spoken for, I'd consider applying.'

'The job is yours, should you choose to accept it,' I said, right back at her. I couldn't believe it: I was flirting with Angela Mathers.

She laughed again, an unbelievably musical sound, but she didn't say anything, she just kept on working the lotion into my shoulders. There was a longish, though not particularly awkward silence before I began to realise that she was almost finished and that I was about to let her go without another word. I cast around desperately for some way to detain her, but my sudden flash of confidence had faded, and now I couldn't think of anything to say.

She patted me gently on the back, and stood up. 'There you go,' she said. 'You'll be right as rain.'

'Thanks,' I said. 'I feel better now.' I stood up too, and

turned towards her, but she had already moved away. 'Can I get you something?' I ventured. 'A drink? Or something?'

She laughed again and shook her head. 'You're incorrigible,' she said, as she headed for the French windows. 'Stay inside, and stay cool,' she sang out in parting; then, with a knowing smile, she added: 'And no more mad dogs and English gin, all right?'

I nodded and, with a last, glorious smile that was meant only for me, she vanished into the sunshine. I wanted to go out too, just to watch her cross the lawn, and see her back safely to her own garden, but I stayed where I was. There was something about that parting smile that made me want to do exactly what she'd told me to do.

Later that evening, before my parents got home, I woke up. I had gone upstairs to lie down for a while, and ended up asleep on my stomach. I was thirsty again, though not for gin. I had no idea what time it was, but I knew the house was empty by the stillness from below, and by the way the sounds from across the way drifted in through my window. The Mathers were in their garden with guests; I could tell from the sounds I could hear, Angela Mathers' bright laugh floating through the dark, the other voices deeper and heavier, like the background characters in a radio drama. I got up and went to the window, still half-naked, the chill of the cool air on my skin, not hurting now, though I knew it would later. From where I stood, I could see her, though she didn't see me, and I watched for as long as I dared, as she talked with her husband and their friends – a grown woman, far away and impossible, just beyond the cherry-laurel hedge. For a moment, I let myself imagine an impossible future, then I went downstairs and fetched a long cold lemonade from the fridge, with plenty of ice.

I saw a documentary once about a group of scientists who spend their entire lives drilling deep into the polar ice cap and analysing the rope-thick, silvery core of it, to find out what the atmosphere was like hundreds of thousands of years ago. They were, in the main, cool, soft-spoken creatures, those Arctic scientists, but you could see in their eyes that something unexpected about their work had touched them deep in the quick of their imaginations, a distance they hadn't anticipated in the ice when they started, a sense of something urgent, besides the cold they endured on a daily basis, or the results they were compiling, building theories of global catastrophe that, for me at least, seemed almost incidental. The ice had affected their bodies, too, making them still and dense, adding a gravitas that I have only ever seen in old black and white films. It had something to do with eternity, and with the cold, this sense I had that each of them was keeping his own secret, not because he wanted to, but because the deeper, more physical knowledge he had achieved, through his work and through grace, could not be put into words. I have never forgotten this programme, though it was, on the surface, a routine science feature on television, *Horizon*, say, or *Equinox*. I remember it for those scientists, for their stillness and for the darkness in their eyes, and I remember the desire I had, watching them handle those beautiful cores of ice, a desire that was as urgent, in its own way, as a real and desperate thirst. What I wanted more than anything was to drink that cold liquid as it dripped from the melting ice-strand, and taste the air of long ago, a trace of prehistory, the cold minerals of origin. What could be more tempting than this? I thought. What could be more necessary than this longing to drink from the purest cold, to gulp down the salty essence of a world before time? As I sat watching them, I could see that these scientists, each in his own way, had tasted that original ice. That was what showed in their eyes and in the way they held themselves. It was a special kind of knowledge they had, a secret that went beyond even the desire to tell. It was the knowledge of ice, the secret of the eternal.

I didn't know, when I was fourteen, that what I loved most was the cold, just as I didn't know, until much later, that the future wasn't really what I was after. Yet what I want most is more than just ice: I love the cold, and high winds, and the first snows, but more than that, I love the chill shiver that fever reveals in the flesh – and so, every year, on the first hot day of summer, I get a medium to bad sunburn. Usually, Cindy is out when it happens, or she's busy with something indoors, so she doesn't catch me out till it's too late. I suppose I shouldn't be surprised that she gets annoyed. She stands looking at me, holding a paintbrush or a bag of groceries, while I sit sheepishly in the kitchen, my shoulders bright red and tingling. Usually I feel a little feverish, as if my whole life is flickering at the border between the real and the imagined but, after the first few minutes, this isn't as unpleasant as Cindy thinks it is. All the while, I want to tell her that I can't help myself, that all of this happens for a reason. I want to say that, somewhere in the back of my mind, I let it happen. I let it happen for love and eternity and a long kinship with the cold. I let it happen for the sensation of putting on a clean white shirt and feeling the shiver run across my back, for the fever that will possess me later, when she is asleep, and for the minutes when I stand awake, half-naked at the window, feeling the cool of the night on my skin, and listening to the dark, for whatever is there, in the quiet of the finite world, millimetres away.

Perfect and Private Things

At two o'clock, on the last Friday of every spring semester, Amanda Bax would make her way along the high street, pausing occasionally for a perfunctory and, in some cases, barely intelligible exchange with a passing colleague or one of her soon-to-be-former students, before disappearing, not just metaphorically but – in something close to a vanishing act that delighted her every time – almost literally, into the florist's on Blackberry Lane. She had been doing this now for thirteen years, but today – which also happened to be her birthday – it felt no less strange and sensual a pleasure than it had the first time around: the little shop, damped down against the summer heat, was, as always, a wall of perfumes and thick, humid shadows, the floor and the long water-stained counter a profusion of roses and stocks and gypsophila, and little Elspeth, white-faced and abstracted, like an illustration from some old fairy tale, busy at the back table in a nest of flower bottles and polypropylene ribbon, assembling bouquets for weddings and exam dinners, her blue-black hair streaked randomly with sap and pollen. By now, Elspeth was used to Amanda's yearly ritual, but she didn't know its purpose: one of those innocents who can only survive in certain more or less isolated vocations, she thought the large bouquet of red roses that Amanda carefully picked out and sent, without a greeting, to a different young man every year, was nothing more than a kindly gesture, a small memento from a dedicated teacher to a particularly intelligent or well-mannered student.

As it happened, nothing could have been further from

the truth, but Amanda had no desire to let Elspeth in on her secret – and she was grateful that the tiny, elf-faced woman who made up her order, in what could only be described as a near-reverent silence, appeared to have no further interest in this transaction than the usual consolation of customer satisfaction. Elspeth, Amanda knew, was religious – she read obscure tracts in her little storeroom-cum-kitchen at the back of the shop when business was slow, and she had once offered up a small, rather faded pamphlet on the Manichean Controversy for Amanda's consideration, back in the early, and less fastidious days of their business together. Yet Amanda did not think – could not, in fact, imagine – her as churchgoing. The idea of Elspeth in a good winter coat and a hat, standing amidst the other worthies in the nave of St Salvator's seemed to Amanda just as unlikely as the idea that she might have a sex life; and, sure enough, their long, if somewhat reserved acquaintance had revealed that Elspeth was, in fact, both a confirmed spinster and something of a spiritual dissenter – on which, had she been disposed to break the terms of their now almost perfect customer-client privilege, Amanda would have been more inclined to congratulate the little florist than to commiserate with her. Amanda was, herself, married, and she had learned long ago that matrimony was not so much the occasion of romantic desire as its final, and inescapable cure.

'These just arrived,' Elspeth said quietly, as she laid out a box of deep red, almost crimson roses. 'I always get something special in for . . . Well . . .' The woman looked at Amanda, with just a hint of dismay in her face.

Amanda nodded. She knew the florist had nothing but good intentions, and that she wasn't trying to start an inappropriate conversation, in order to pry. 'They're lovely,' she said. 'Two dozen of those would be perfect.'

'And gypsophila?' The florist looked up at her enquiringly, then immediately bowed her head.

Amanda thought she detected the smallest trace of a blush in that chalk-white face. She didn't like the smell of gypsophila, but they added something – a neither-here-nor-there quality that contrasted sharply with the blood-coloured roses – and she always had a little, just to lighten the bouquet. 'Oh, yes,' she said, her voice no more than a satisfied murmur, directed mostly to herself. 'Most definitely. *Gypsophila.*'

Sending the flowers was a break in her normal day-to-day routine, but it was nothing compared to the ritual she observed directly upon leaving the shop. It was a ritual that, for several reasons, she preferred to observe alone – usually the simplest thing in the world to arrange except that, on this particular morning, halfway through breakfast, Simon had suddenly asked, quite out of the blue, if she wanted to meet up after his last tutorial of the year and go to the Westport for a drink. He had made this sugges-tion while she was about to pour the tea and, for one delicious moment, she considered spilling the hot liquid over his outstretched hand and the sleeve of his natty houndstooth jacket – quite accidentally, of course – before pulling herself together and fashioning a more or less unlikely excuse. Fortunately, the one *good* thing about marriage, after it passed the ten-year stage at least, was that excuses no longer needed to be plausible. Simon knew that Amanda wasn't seeing anyone else – had he considered the idea even for a moment, he would only have found it amusing – and it was easier on them both if she claimed a prior 'postgraduate pastoral meeting' or an impending deadline, rather than simply admitting what she knew for certain, and suspected that *he* suspected, which was, not to put too fine a point on it, that she would rather stand up to her neck in slurry for a week than sit with him for a perfunctory birthday drink in some café-bar while he eyed up the waitress.

Still, it had been a close call. If he'd arranged something
that involved someone else – some kind of celebration
with Matt and Sarah, for example – she wouldn't have
been able to get out of it so easily, and she couldn't help
lingering for a moment over his basic lack of tact. Didn't
he *know* how their life was organised by now? What could
possibly have prompted him to suggest they go out together
– *by themselves*? Didn't he understand the unspoken rules
that, as far as she had understood, they had contrived, in
a tacit mutual exercise in trial and error, to build conven-
iently separate lives? For a long moment, after he had
returned to his copy of *The Times Ed*, she considered him
with something close to rage. Or not rage, so much as
loathing. She had married Simon when he was a rising
star in academic circles, but he had stopped rising long
ago and settled, not altogether deliberately, for comfort.
Now he worked in the Cultural Studies Department of
the respectable but unexciting new university where she,
the perennial academic wife, had taken a part-time post
teaching modern poetry. She had written her doctoral
thesis on Weldon Kees and enjoyed reciting the opening
lines of his heartbreaking elegy 'The Smiles of the Bathers'
to her startled students when they first arrived for her US
Poetry in the Twentieth Century module:

> The smiles of the bathers fade as they leave the
>   water,
> And the lover feels sadness fall as it ends, as he
>   leaves his love.
> The scholar, closing his book as the midnight
>   clock strikes, is hollow and old;
> The pilot's relief on landing is no release.
> These perfect and private things, walling us in,
>   have imperfect and public endings –
> Water and wind and flight, remembered words and
>   the act of love

> Are but interruptions. And the world, like a beast,
>   impatient and quick,
> Waits only for those who are dead. No death for
>   you. You are involved.

She loved that poem and, with this untimely and unex-
plained recital – followed immediately, after the briefest
pause for effect, by a taking of the class roll – established
herself as an eccentric among the students, and so, if not
liked, then at least regarded. Eventually, she had drifted
into teaching full-time and, during the occasional unexpectedly stimulating class, she actually enjoyed it, becoming
more caught up in her professional existence with each
new failure in her marriage, till all she and Simon had
in common were New Year's parties with a handful of
similarly faded colleagues and the occasional dinner with
Matt and Sarah, who both worked in Art History and
were too wrapped up in their research interests – abstract
expressionism and pre-Columbian pottery, respectively
– to notice that their closest friends could barely sit in
the same room together for more than a couple of hours
at a time. What couldn't be concealed, however, was the
long-term hiatus in Simon's professional standing, and his
recent lack of worthwhile publications. For a long time,
he had traded on the reputation of his one good book
– a more or less Marxist study of Robert Louis Stevenson
– but that flame had burnt out long ago and all that
remained was the confidence he had acquired during his
brief but, to him, utterly deserved period of high standing.
The book's thesis – that RLS was, in effect, Scotland's
Goethe – had been cobbled together from a close reading
of Marshall Berman, a probable misinterpretation of *The
Strange Case of Dr Jekyll and Mr Hyde*, and youthful arrogance,
and went something along the lines that, with the Jekyll/
Hyde paradigm, Stevenson had gone one better on
the Faust/Mephistopheles pairing, claiming that, in

response to the high period of modernity, what had been a post-Enlightenment vision of intellect set against and complemented by raw power had been resolved by RLS into an essentially schizoid model, where the hero, instead of being assisted by some supernatural force from without, was left alone with himself, divided, perhaps, between intellect and id, but divided *inside* the single, riven soul of a truly modern man, for whom human nature has become at once a monster and a liberator. So far, Amanda supposed, so run of the mill, but Simon had then cobbled together a Marxist interpretation of this schismatic self that, apparently, nobody had ever thought of before – perhaps because most people had better things to do with their waking hours. Of course, in the early days, she had tried to see the brilliance of her new husband's thesis, but she had never been altogether convinced and now, a decade and a half later, she had come to the conclusion that the only regret she had – not just in this case, but in so many others along the way – was that she had too often allowed herself the luxury of misplaced loyalty.

But loyalty, of any kind, was a thing of the past now. *Now*, her anonymous bouquet duly despatched, she was ducking in from the May sunshine to the dim, beer-scented bar of the Withies Tavern for the second half of her yearly ceremony of perfect and private things. The roses were on their way to the boy she had chosen this year – a tall, skinny Mancunian named Tim, who had stood with her for just a moment too long once or twice in the quad, rambling about William Carlos Williams – and now it was time to relax into the warm, slow lull of forgetting that had become her once-yearly pleasure. It had taken her a long time to understand that, when it came to romance, she preferred certain varieties of subtle pain – physical, when that was possible, emotional and psychological when it was not – to any conventional notion of happiness. She had, in fact, refused to give the idea of happiness anything more than passing consideration: it had immediately struck her as an illusion, a sorry bribe offered by social convention – that complex, mediocre Authorised Version of life and love – to divert its subjects from other possibilities, possibilities that Amanda had explored, alone and occasionally with others, enough to understand that, for her at least, the unnamed alternative to this insipid happiness consisted of blood and fire and absence in more or less equal measure. Naturally, she had never conducted these experiments in pain with the boys who, like Tim, drifted through her poetry classes, too self-absorbed or too inarticulate to claim the prize that they sensed might just be available behind the ironic facade she maintained through the occasional intense conversation after class, a prize that, had they been able to claim it, would have cut them to the quick. She knew that. Fifteen years of being married to Simon had made her dangerous, too hungry to be left alone for too long with anything that could all too easily, in a certain slant of light, begin to look like prey. All that longing had to be contained; all that desire had to be ritualised. A bewildered boy called to the door in his PJs, hungover from a post-exam party, to take delivery of two dozen blood-coloured roses; a secret held in her mind in much the same way as the one thorn she would break from a rose stem and clutch to her palm as she left the shop; a glass of malt whisky in the dim bar of the Withies, among men she didn't know. That was what she had, and it almost sufficed.

This year, however – this year, for the first time ever – there *was* someone she knew in the bar of the Withies. He was sitting at a table in the middle of the room, part of a large group that included several boys and a few girls, all obviously fellow students, though none of the others was from any of the classes that Amanda taught. They were the only other customers in the bar, and they had dragged chairs from the tables close by to make a wide, untidy circle around a sea of beer bottles and half-eaten packets of crisps. A few looked round when she came in, but Tim had his back to her, and she was grateful for that. Still, she hesitated, nonetheless, before she made up her mind and walked over to the bar. There, quietly, but firmly, she ordered a whisky from the large, horse-faced landlord whose name, she had once heard, was Bill. She didn't *know* the man, naturally, but she could always tell from his expression that he remembered her from previous visits. Maybe this was part of his inner calendar: early summer, strange woman comes in, drinks one or two whiskies, then leaves. The Withies wasn't a pub generally patronised by students or academics − that was why she had chosen it − so she probably stood out enough for him to recall her face. Or her manner, perhaps. Usually, she was happy, usually she felt strong and confident, someone in charge of her life and going about it with a certain relish. Today, however, she didn't feel confident at all. She felt studied. She felt looked at − not just by this man, but by the entire room. Still, she ordered the whisky, paid for it and started towards her usual place − the table by the door, where she could sit with her back to the bar and look out at the flowering shrubs in the walled garden − because she was determined not to let her ritual be spoiled. She wouldn't stay long, perhaps − just one whisky this time − but she would do what she needed to do and, when it was done, she would catch a taxi home and open the bottle of wine she had left to chill in the fridge. And she would be damned if she let anything divert her.

Tim still had his back to her as she crossed over to the table by the door, but one of the other boys looked up and, as if making her out for the first time, gave her an odd look, a smile that wasn't quite right, something approaching, but not altogether, an actual smirk. She didn't know who he was, but there was something in that half-smile that made her look away a little too quickly, so he knew she had noticed him, and she hadn't wanted that at all. She moved quickly to her table and sat down, her back to the group; then she drank some of the whisky right away, not lingering over it a moment as she usually did, but gulping it, rather, the ice butting at her teeth, the taste too sudden and too warm in her throat. She didn't know *why* she was upset. Tim knew nothing at all about her yearly ritual and she wasn't besotted by him, like some lovestruck girl. Nevertheless, she was surprised to realise that she was *very* upset indeed and she had to allow herself a long moment to calm down, before she took another sip. Only then did she look up – and that was when she realised that Tim had seen her and was watching her, that he had, perhaps, been watching her for several moments, with a detached, even impassive expression. He didn't say anything, and his face remained still, but he kept on looking at her for another long moment, before one of the others spoke and he looked away, his eyes alighting on the girl's face as if he had suddenly found something he'd lost and had been trying to find for the longest time. Amanda couldn't make out what the girl had said, but she was smiling and, after a moment, Tim laughed.

Amanda looked away. She didn't want to hear that laugh, or see him like that, with a girl he liked, among friends, celebrating the end of exams. Now and then, she would imagine him drinking, or at a party, she would even imagine him out with friends, but those others were never very clearly defined. They were amorphous, anonymous, the merest background to the leading actor in her fantasy. Not that she fantasised often; that wasn't the point of this ritual. It wasn't about the boys; it was about *her*. It was about the ritual she had created, a form of discipline, a process by which she entertained and, at the same time, purged herself of certain impulses, going through the stages of something clear and well defined so that this year's Tim, or Andy, or Greg could begin the long process, not of fading from her memory so much as merging into the massed weight of those who had gone before. She didn't *want* them. She didn't want anything to happen with them. She didn't want to take these boys home to her bed, or creep from their rooms at three in the morning, mussed and sticky and stupidly illumined with guilt or lust. This had always been a game to her, and that game had only one true player.

Now, though, the game had been interrupted. A rule had been broken and, as she finished the whisky and rose to her feet, she felt cheated, just a little – cheated and deceived, somehow, though by whom she couldn't say. Not by Tim, or his friends, not by the landlord, certainly, and not by anyone she could have named. Yet, even as she made her way to the door – not looking at Tim's group as she passed, though not too obviously averting her gaze either – she couldn't altogether dispel that sensation of having been tricked, and she knew that she wouldn't be able to redeem the ritual until she got herself a taxi and headed for home. She still didn't know *why* she felt so upset – but she was, and it seemed to her that she had given something away, she had let something become visible, or rather tangible, that should have been kept concealed. Not from those boys, not from the landlord, not from the world, but from herself. Something had dawned on her that made her feel awkward and ordinary. It was a feeling she didn't want to have, an understanding she didn't want to acknowledge. She couldn't name it – it wasn't really about sex and it certainly wasn't about love either. It was something else, something more basic and needful – and it seemed to her, as she walked to the far end of Church Street and got into the first available taxi, that it was about touch, if anything: touch and then, inevitably, what touch led to – and that was what made it so frightening. If one of those boys had ever thought to reach out and touch her face, she told herself, if he had just brushed a stray lock of hair from her eyes as they stood talking in the quad, she would have dissolved into the moment and let go of the stupid grief she had carried for so long – so long and yet so lightly, it seemed, a light and steady and habitual dismay, part of what she was to herself and, so, a subtle trapdoor in the world through which, with the least contact, she and whoever touched her might fall forever, into the pleasurable pain that, presumably, they *both* secretly wanted. A pain that could not be ritualised with roses and whisky, a pain that could not be kept from the world, but demanded to be celebrated, openly. It would never happen, of course, she knew that, or at least, she told herself she knew it, staring silently out of the car window at the last of the houses sliding by, and then at the water meadows, and then at her own house, set in the tidy garden that Simon paid a young man with a nose ring and the most absurd acne to keep in immaculate condition, even though they never used it. She told herself that she had always known that nothing would ever happen and she reminded herself once again that she didn't *want* anything to happen – just as she knew, now, having paid the taxi driver and walked, steadily, to her all too familiar front door, that the only real pleasure remaining to her was an ordered solitude that, from time to time, would present itself as a gift – just as it did right then, quite unexpectedly, in the moment when she stepped inside and stood quietly in the hall, sensing that the house was, for some reason, mercifully empty. She didn't know where Simon was – he'd indicated at breakfast that he would be back by mid-afternoon – but at that moment everything brightened and she walked straight to the kitchen to pour herself some Chablis from the bottle she had left cooling in the fridge, and she didn't notice until her glass was full and she went through to the last buttery sunshine streaming in through the windows of the dining room, that someone

97

had left a huge bouquet of roses on the time-weathered table just inside the door – two dozen of them, blood-red, but lightened here and there with a few strands of gypsophila, the dense, almost black thorns just visible through the plastic wrapping.

GODWIT

Back in the old days, before Fat Stan went to prison, we used to go out on the Sands every afternoon, to watch the seabirds and hunt for godwit. There were all kinds of waders out there, curlews and turnstones and sandpipers, all flitting about from place to place and making soft wheeping sounds when you got too close, but if you found a good spot and sat dead still, you could watch for ages, while they strutted back and forth along the tide line, probing the mud with their long curved beaks. They only flew when they had to, but that didn't matter, because I liked the way they walked. You could tell they were watching for danger all the time, but they still acted like they owned the place, strolling around with their wings behind their backs, all full of themselves, like old-fashioned banker types out for a constitutional. They evolved differently, Stan said, and some of them only stayed for the winter before they flitted off somewhere else to breed and such. Most of the types we saw were pretty common, but now and then we would glimpse this one bird, which Stan said was a black-tailed godwit, and that was rare. He also told me that in olden times those birds were prized for their meat – better than anything, even swan, it said in this book he'd read – and he was determined to hunt one down and try it out.

I hadn't reckoned on Stan knowing so much about wildlife, and I wondered if maybe he was having me on, so I went down the library one day and looked up the black-tailed godwit in this big *Field Guide to British Birds* they had in the reference section. I was half-expecting it to be something completely different and, to start with, I thought Stan was talking out of his arse, because the bird in the main picture was sort of orangey-brown looking and much more colourful than the ones on the Sands. But then I had to admit he was right, sure enough, because that big picture was the black-tailed godwit in its summer plumage, and there was another one, further down the page, that showed how it looked in winter. Of course, that godwit in the picture looked cleaner and more graceful than the one we'd seen on the Sands, but then things always do look better in books, all in their true colours, like they would be if the world was perfect and, anyway, you could still see that they were identical, when you made allowances for real life. It gave me a new respect for Stan, I have to say, him knowing that kind of thing. Not that I ever *disrespected* him, but there were times when you could see how unlucky he was, and when bad luck shows, it makes you think less of a person, because you can't help wondering if they brought it on themselves somehow.

Fat Stan wasn't so fat when he got his name. A bit pudgy, maybe, but not obese, like he turned out later. What happened was, there were two Stanleys in our class and the other one was about six feet tall and very skinny. I mean, really, stick-thin. My cousin Alan said, if you sneezed next to him, the boy would fall to pieces, he was just so much skin and bone. That Stanley had long blond hair in school, but he went bald, pretty much overnight, when he was sixteen. Nobody could explain it. After that, of course, everybody called him Baldy, but in school he was Thin Stan, which meant that the Stan I went around with, my best friend since I was seven years old, became Fat Stan. My name was Jamie and it still is. Wee Jamie sometimes, and sometimes Mad Jamie, because I've got some mental problems, but it's not like I ever had a proper nickname.

Which might be lucky, because Stan's nickname had a

real effect on him, and over the years he put on more and more weight, till he got to be the obese person he is today. That's what they call it, *obese*, which always makes me think of massive lardy women lolling around in front of the telly with a bag of Doritos in one hand and a gallon of ice cream in the other, but if you knew Stan, if you really paid attention, you could see that he was pretty graceful for someone so big. I remember watching him at a party, once, he was out on the dance floor with this pretty, red-haired girl I used to fancy, and he was so light on his feet, so full of grace and energy, moving around the room like a real dancer, with that big happy smile on his face that people have when they're doing something unexpected. Caroline Mason — that was the girl's name. She was Haggis Mason's little sister, though you'd never have thought it. Haggis used to deal stolen goods out of the Crow's Nest, and you would see him around town with his dog, a big German shepherd bitch called Kim. According to Stan, Haggis used to give Kim half a tab of microdot from time to time, then take her out to the park so she could run around. Haggis would drop a couple of tabs too, trying to see the world through his dog's eyes — and Stan said that, one time, Kim had gone haywire and chased Haggis up a tree, so he'd had to sit there for hours, with the dog running round and round in crazy circles below, her big saucer-eyes staring up at him like she had no idea who he was. I don't know how Stan knew this, but I wouldn't be surprised if it was Haggis who told him — because when you first met him, Stan came over as somebody you could trust. I mean, I always thought I could talk to him about anything, even about my mental problems, and he'd listen, but he wouldn't pass anything on, and that really mattered to me, because I didn't want anybody else knowing what went on inside my head when I was like that.

All that changed after we met Zoë-Anne, though. I mean,

I told him how I felt about her, but I knew it was a mistake as soon as I got the words out. Course, I didn't know that he liked her too, because he's a really proud guy and he always pretended he wasn't interested. 'That's jailbait,' he would say, whenever she came around. 'That little girl will get you arrested, before you know it,' he'd say, and then he'd turn away, like that was all there was to say. I didn't care, though. Nobody had ever liked me before, Zoë-Anne was the first and for a while I thought something was going to happen between us. I should have known better, though, because I'm just like Fat Stan, bad luck is written all over my face, and after what happened with Eddie Mac, Zoë-Anne just disappeared. Right now I've got no idea where she is, which shouldn't have been a surprise, because I never had any idea where she came from either. I asked her a couple of times, but she just shrugged. 'What difference does it make?' she said, and that worried me, because of what Stan said about her being so young.

Zoë-Anne found me and Stan one February afternoon, as we were coming in out of the fog. I don't know why she was there – if Stan was right about her age, she ought to have been in school – but she probably noticed us coming up the beach and got curious to see what we were doing. Which was that we'd been hunting godwit, but we didn't tell her that. She was a pretty girl, with short dark hair and really blue eyes, and she had a bright, sarcastic look that made me think of the actress in one of those screwball comedies Mam used to watch on Saturday afternoons. The look that said she knew what you were about to say even before you opened your mouth, and it didn't matter anyway, because she'd heard it all before. I liked that look, I don't know why. Even though it made me think of those old Hollywood actresses, there was something kind of French about it too, and I thought that was sexy, because when you looked closer, you could see she was just a kid, and it was all a bluff, really. So I liked her right from the start, though I wouldn't have dared to ask her out, not if she hadn't started it.

She didn't say anything till we came across the strip of dune-grass that divided the town from the Sands. Then she spoke – and I noticed that she looked right at me, as if it was just the two of us. She wasn't smiling or anything, she was just curious, in a bored sort of way, but she was talking to me, and I reckoned she was just pretending to be bored. I also noticed that her eyes were really blue, like the colour of cornflowers and that looked kind of spooky, with her jet-black hair. 'What are you doing?' she said.

I wanted to say something, but I couldn't. I was tongue-tied, because her eyes were so blue and because she hadn't been talking to Stan, she had only talked to me. Stan glanced at her sideways, then he turned and shook his head. 'I didn't know it was school holidays already,' he said.

Zoë-Anne didn't even look at him, though. She just kept her eyes on me. 'What's your name, mate?' she said. 'You look familiar.'

Stan gave a little snort and carried on walking, but I stopped right next to her, just a couple of feet away. 'I'm Jamie,' I said, but when I spoke, my voice sounded funny, and I couldn't say anything else.

Zoë-Anne smiled then. 'What are you doing out here, Jamie?' she said. 'Don't you know the Sands are dangerous?'

I shook my head. 'Nah,' I said. 'It's not dangerous. Not if you know where to go.' And it was true, more or less. I mean, everybody knew you could come to grief out there, but Stan and me, we'd always loved the Sands, ever since we were kids. It was a place to escape to, to get away from the rest of the world. We'd go out in all weathers, wandering about in the fog or in the pale, watery sunlight, or just sitting on the rocks beyond the headland, smoking dope when we had some and staring out into the dimming tide. One time, we dropped some acid and went out into the mist: it was pretty thin that day, not like the big fogs that rolled in all the time, but it was still difficult to see and, twenty yards out, we lost our bearings, so we had to go by instinct towards the far side of the bay, stepping delicately over the treacherous wet sand, trying to avoid the places where you could sink up to your thighs in a matter of seconds, or wading waist-deep in the water where we had no choice but to navigate one of the deep channels that criss-cross the bay. I wasn't scared, though. Everybody knows that the Sands are dangerous, a couple of people have even died out there, but that day, we were invulnerable. We were hypersensitive to everything and we knew exactly where to place our feet, exactly what spots to avoid. We walked right across the bay and we passed through huge flocks of birds, and they didn't mind us at all. They didn't get scared, and they didn't fly away, they just watched as we passed them by, light-footed and ever so tender, like ghosts from some former age, out wandering in the mist. By the time we got to the other side, we were wet to the bone and covered in silt and mud, but we didn't care.

After Zoë-Anne turned up, though, we didn't do anything like that again. She made me happy for a while, but I could tell Stan didn't like her, or I thought he didn't anyway. That first time, he just ignored her, and I didn't know what else to say, so we just stood for a couple of minutes, looking out into the fog and pretending we weren't embarrassed. We were, though – or I was anyway and, after a while, I said goodbye and went after Stan. I walked slowly, I even went backwards for a few steps, in case she said something else. She didn't, though. She just stood there watching me go and, eventually, I had to turn around and look where I was walking and, once I did, I was too embarrassed to turn back again, so I didn't see where she went after that. I felt weird, to tell the truth, because I thought she would go off and forget about me and I didn't think I could stand it, not seeing her again. I kept on walking, though, and when I finally did look back, at the far edge of the car park, she was gone, and there was nothing to see but sand and fog.

Stan and me didn't go down to the shore for a couple of days, but when we did, Zoë-Anne was waiting, in the same place we'd seen her before, standing at the edge of the car park, gazing out towards the sea. It was a fine day, for the time of year: the air was cool but there was sunlight spilling over the Sands in long runs between the cloud shadows, and there were hundreds of birds wandering about in great flocks, each group concentrated in its own area, stint and dunlin on the hard, open mud, oystercatchers, turnstones and, out in the tide, way out on the other side of that wide expanse of sun and shadow, I thought I could see some black-tailed godwit, the ones that Stan said were so good to eat. Stan had brought a net someone had given him, to see if he could rig it up and catch something, but it was stowed away in a white plastic shopping bag, so Zoë-Anne didn't see it. I was glad about that, all of a sudden. It hadn't seemed cruel to me before, hunting for godwit. Stan said it was the same as eating a chicken, and we ate chicken, didn't we? Now, though, with her standing in front of me, a funny little smile on her face like she was pleased to see us, I started to think maybe it wasn't right.

Zoë-Anne was wearing a white blouse and a dark-green skirt, which I realised was the same thing she'd been wearing the last time we saw her – and that meant Stan was right, she was just a kid skiving off from school. That green was exactly the same colour as the St Barnabas uniform, and only sixth-formers didn't have to wear it, so that meant she was sixteen or under. Stan had said, after the last time, that she was probably about fourteen, fifteen at the most, and that I'd better not get interested in her, but I hadn't argued with him, because there was nothing to argue about. I mean, it wasn't like we were going out or anything. It wasn't like we were having sex. She was just this pretty girl who liked to hang about the Sands, watching to see what people got up to. That was all. She was only being friendly, and there was no harm in that. Now, she came up to me and gave me that little smile, to show she was pleased we'd come. 'Hiya,' she said, and she was talking to me again, not to Stan, just like the last time.

'Haven't you got a home to go to?' Stan said. He didn't say it nasty, though. He was just looking out for me, because he thought I'd get in trouble, and I suppose I could see his point, not because I was planning anything, but because of what people might say.

Zoë-Anne smiled sweetly. 'I wasn't talking to you,' she said. 'I was talking to *Jamie*.' The way she said my name, it was like we'd known each other for years, and I felt that weird happiness coming over me again, just like before.

Stan gave her a sarcastic grin. 'Is that right?' he said.

Zoë-Anne grinned right back at him. '*Absolutely*,' she said.

Stan hovered a moment, and I could tell that he was trying to think of a clever put-down; then he gave up and moved away. I could see that he planned to go out there and set up the net, and he wanted me to help him, but I stayed where I was, next to Zoë-Anne at the edge of the tarmac. I didn't think he stood much chance of catching anything, but you never knew. He took a few more steps, then he noticed I'd stopped and he turned round to see where I was. 'Well?' he said. 'Are you coming or not?'

'Where are you going, anyway?' Zoë-Anne said, her blue eyes on the bag.

'Nowhere that's any business of yours,' Stan said. His mouth tightened and he gave me a look. 'Come on, Jamie,' he said, and his voice was hard now, like somebody talking to a kid who's about to do something naughty.

And it wasn't like I wanted to show him up or anything, but just at that moment, I realised that I didn't want to go out on the Sands either. I wanted to stay there, next to Zoë-Anne, and feel that weird happy feeling. So I didn't move. I just stayed put. 'You go,' I said. 'I'm going to stop here for a bit.'

I could see he wasn't happy, then. He stood awhile, staring at me like I was having one of my weird spells, and I thought for a minute he'd come over and try and force me to go with him. But he didn't say anything else, he just gave me a funny little smile, like he'd expected this to happen and he was sorry that it had. Then he turned away and started off across the Sands, walking slowly into the wet February sunlight.

I know this sounds stupid, but that next week or so was the happiest time of my life. Nothing really happened, but I saw Zoë-Anne every day, even on the weekends, and we started going for walks together, just me and her. We would meet at the bus stop on Milburn Street – she wouldn't tell me where her house was, and she never let me walk her home afterwards – then we would go walking in the abbey grounds, reading the names off the headstones of master chefs and women who'd died in childbirth a hundred years ago. Or we would wander around the castle grounds, not touching, not even talking half the time, like people who had known each other for years and felt so comfortable together they didn't have to say a word. We didn't go out to the Sands, so I didn't see Stan for over a week, which was odd, because we'd been mates forever. It was just me and Zoë-Anne. I'm not saying we were going out together, boyfriend girlfriend, but I was happy, just standing next to her, aware of her body and her eyes and the sound of her voice. I was happy, and I felt almost lucky, which hadn't seemed possible before and I didn't want to lose that feeling.

In the end, though, I ran into Stan in town and I could see right away that he was in bad shape. That was what happened with him, sometimes. If you left him to his own devices, he'd go out, get ripped, start mouthing off at somebody or trying to move in on some regular bloke's girlfriend, and all hell would break loose. He never did that when he was straight, but when he had a drink or a taste on him, he'd go all out of control. Of course, I didn't know it then but I should have guessed that he'd got himself into worse trouble than usual this time – and that was why he looked so pathetic, wandering around town in a grubby T-shirt all covered with grease and pizza stains. I was on my way to meet Zoë-Anne, so I didn't really want to get dragged into his mess, but when I saw him like that, I didn't have any choice but to stop and talk and then, before I knew it, we were arranging to meet up later, out on the Sands. I even told him I was bringing Zoë-Anne, but he didn't bat an eyelid. He just said that he'd see me later, at the usual place.

He didn't tell me about Eddie Mac, though. He didn't say he'd helped himself to the guy's drugs, or that Eddie was out looking for him. He just let me believe that he'd been on a bender, and that was that. So I went to the bus stop on Milburn Street and picked up Zoë-Anne, then the two of us walked down to the Sands, to see that he was all right. She didn't really want to go, but I'd known Stan too long to leave him hanging out to dry. So we made our way slowly to the usual place and, when we got there, we found Fat Stan wandering up and down the beach, his head down, pretending he hadn't seen us.

'What's he doing?' Zoë-Anne said.

'He's embarrassed,' I said.

'Why?'

'Because he messed up,' I said.

She didn't say anything then, she just sat down on the rocks and I sat down next to her, waiting for Stan to come to his senses. Which was exactly where we were when Eddie Mac arrived: two people sitting on the rocks, watching Stan stomp up and down the beach, like some sad couple with a dysfunctional, slightly crazed child. By the time Eddie got there, a thick fog had rolled in, thicker than I'd seen it in months, and that was pretty, but all in all, it was a fairly sad occasion and, even though she was being good about it, I knew Zoë-Anne didn't like playing nursemaid.

Meanwhile, Stan stayed out by himself, not looking in our direction, but running in and out of the fog like he was hoping that, if he did it just once too often, he would disappear – and, the truth was, we were pretty tired of just sitting there, being ignored, when Eddie Mac turned up and stood at the edge of the sand, his eyes fixed on Stan, who was still fifty yards further down the beach with his back to us. A moment later, and we would probably have been gone already. It was just our bad luck that we hadn't got fed up sooner.

Eddie came to within five yards of where we were sitting, then he turned to Zoë-Anne, looked her up and down, and shook his head. 'Please tell me this isn't your girlfriend, James,' he said.

I didn't say anything. I was trying to make out that I didn't care about Zoë-Anne because, that way, Eddie might leave her alone, but the truth was, I already knew he wasn't really talking to me. He was talking to Zoë-Anne. I shot her a warning look, but it was too late.

'Go fuck yourself,' was all she said, only she said it the way Claudette Colbert would have done in one of those old screwball comedies, assuming Claudette Colbert had been allowed to use language like that. Which, any other time, would have brought Eddie down on me – because if some girl crossed you, you didn't take it out on her, you kicked the fuck out of her boyfriend. On this particular occasion, though, Eddie was distracted – distracted and suddenly alarmed as Stan, who must have been watching us all along out of the corner of his eye, did exactly what nobody expected him to do – which was to run straight into the fog and keep going. Eddie Mac started running too, then, but by the time he got to where Stan had been, there was no sign of anyone and, suddenly realising that he was on dangerous ground, Eddie pulled up sharp and stood staring into the fog. Like I said, everybody round here knows how hazardous the Sands can be, especially in bad weather, and I *know* it took him by surprise that Stan had gone out there, into certain danger. People had got hopelessly lost in conditions like that and they had never come back. One guy had been out there for hours, and all the time the rescue team knew he was just ten yards away, more or less, only they couldn't find him in the fog. They could hear him calling for help, and they tried working their way towards the sound, but they didn't get there until it was too late. That was the kind of thing that could happen out there. One false step and the Sands would claim you forever, sucking you down into the dark and snuffing you out in a matter of minutes.

One thing you had to say about Eddie was, he wasn't stupid. And maybe, that day, he was hoping Stan wasn't that stupid either, because he waited a long time for him to re-emerge, gazing into the fog and hoping the Sands didn't claim his prey before he did. And today, after all that's happened, I admit that I wish Fat Stan hadn't come back from the fog that afternoon. I wish I could say that he walked a few yards further than he'd ever walked before and just melted away into all that whiteness, because that would have been the happiest ending any of us could have managed. People shouldn't have to die, or go to prison for nothing; they should be allowed to go out and disappear when the right moment comes. I can't say how long Stan stayed out there, wandering about with the birds on the other side of the fog, but he stayed long enough for

Eddie to give up and wander back up the shore, annoyed that he'd got sand on his shoes for nothing.

Eddie didn't even look at us as he went by. Probably he would have shoved me about a bit, if I'd been on my own, but Zoë-Anne being there seemed to embarrass him now. 'You tell that fat bastard I'm going to beat him to pulp if he doesn't pay me what he owes,' he said, as he came up the beach and crossed the line of dune-grass between the Sands and the car park, but he kept his eyes dead ahead and he didn't even pause as he walked by. I didn't say anything, and I didn't move and neither did Zoë-Anne. Then, when she was sure Eddie was gone, she turned to me. She was doing her best not to look upset, for my sake more than anything, but I knew she was – and I knew, then, that Stan was right. She was just a kid, even if she did have a touch of Claudette Colbert about her. 'Nice friends you've got,' she said.

I shook my head. 'Eddie Mac's no friend of mine,' I said, only noticing how stupid that sounded when the words were already out.

'I don't mean him,' she said. Then she lifted herself wearily from the rock where she'd been sitting. 'Anyway,' she said. 'I'd better get going.' She looked at me. 'Are you coming or are you stopping here?'

I looked out towards the fog. 'I'd better wait,' I said. 'See if Stan's all right.'

Zoë-Anne nodded. 'I thought you'd say that,' she said, then she walked away across the tarmac, towards town.

I should have walked her back. I knew that. Eddie could have been hanging around still and, even though I would have been useless to her, I should have made the offer. I didn't, though. I waited for Stan. It was almost an hour before he emerged from the fog and, when he did, he wasn't saying much. He was embarrassed, I suppose, that he'd run away. He was embarrassed, and I guess he must have been angry, though I couldn't see why he would have been angry with me. He was, though. He didn't ask where Zoë-Anne was, or whether she was OK and he didn't want to know what had happened after he ran off. He just walked up the beach to where I was standing and gave me a nasty look.

'Are you all right?' I said.

He shook his head, like it was my fault. 'No,' he said. 'I'm not all right.'

I had nothing to say to that, of course, because I knew he was scared. He was trapped in a corner and there was no way out of it that I could see. People like me and Stan didn't mess around with people like Eddie Mac. You steered clear of him, if you could and, if you didn't that was your funeral. Stan knew that, everybody did – and that was what I couldn't understand. I couldn't understand why he'd got mixed up with people like that and, even though I knew it was a mistake to say anything, I wanted him to tell me why.

Before I could ask the question, though, he spoke again, his voice thin and cold, and different from anything I'd ever heard from him before. 'I've got to do something about this,' he said. 'I'm not going down to some twat like Eddie. Not in a million years.' He looked me in the eyes and I could see that he was waiting for something from me, so I nodded. I didn't really believe he would do anything, though. I didn't think he had it in him to go after Eddie Mac personally. He wasn't one of the hard boys, or anything like that. He was just Stan. So it wasn't until later that I saw how much I underestimated his pride that afternoon. I could see that he was scared, and I knew frightened people will do stupid things sometimes, but I know now that it was pride that made him go after Eddie with a blade. Pride, or self-respect, if you want to call it that. The judge said later that Stan was just a street thug with a knife, callously robbing a young man of his life and his future, but that wasn't how it was. It was pride, and fear, and shame, in more or less equal measure, the same pride and fear and shame that anybody would have felt, if they had been in Stan's place that day.

I didn't see him again after that. Not till the trial. I went looking for Zoë-Anne the next day, hoping she'd come back to the Sands and then, when she wasn't there, I walked to the bus stop where we'd met for our first date. It was raining pretty hard, a cold, greasy rain that stuck to my face and hair, but I stood for two hours on Milburn Street, waiting for her to show. Then, when she didn't, I walked back to my mam's house and had a hot bath. The next day was Friday, which was always a big night at the Raven, where Eddie Mac hung out, doing deals in the car park or standing at the bar watching the girls on the dance floor. I'd been there a few times and I'd noticed how bored and unhappy all those hard boys looked, trying to look mean and making smart comments to any talent that went by, and I'd wondered if they weren't just lonely and a bit scared themselves, trying not to put a foot wrong, making out that they were so tough. Eddie Mac was just like the rest of them, if you ask me, just a scared bloke trying to look like he owned the whole world. He didn't deserve to die, though. Nobody deserves to die like that, and Stan shouldn't have done what he did.

The one mercy was that Eddie didn't really see it coming. Nobody did, and nobody even registered what was happening till it was all over. The Raven was noisy that night so it probably looked like Stan had come out of nowhere when he walked up to where Eddie was waiting at the bar and stabbed him twice in the face and neck. Everybody said it happened so quickly, they didn't even know it was Stan who did it. In the confusion afterwards, some people even thought it had been the other way round, and that Stan had been the one who got cut, because everybody had heard that Eddie Mac and Stan had a beef, and they all thought Stan's card was marked. Whatever they imagined they saw, though, nobody did anything to stop Fat Stan when he turned around and walked back towards the door with the wet knife in his hand, a blank look on his face like nothing had happened. When Eddie Mac went down, there was the usual fuss you get after a fight – some girl standing nearby with blood on her dress, screaming, Eddie's mates milling around trying to figure out what had happened, Gerry from behind the bar shouting for someone to switch on the lights while three lads picked Eddie up bodily and carried him outside. God knows why. Maybe they thought he needed the air, maybe it was just so he wouldn't have to bleed out on the Raven floor, among the fag ends and spilt beer. They say Eddie took a while to die, and his mouth was moving the whole time, like he was trying to say something, but nobody could make out what it was. One guy told me afterwards that he was asking for his mother, but nobody knows for sure and I seem to remember that Eddie and his mam weren't even that close.

Everybody agrees, though, that he was there for several minutes before the ambulance came, laid out on the steps that led in to the dance hall, all the girls spilling out of the room to look at him, the smell of Friday-night perfume thick on the air, girls from the factory where his mam worked straining to see, girls he'd known in school, girls who had lived along the street from him and gone out with him a couple of times before deciding he wasn't right, all coming round so he could look up into their faces, while Gerry tried to staunch the flow of blood with a wad of bar towels. When the ambulance finally got to him, Eddie Mac was dead, or close to dead and there was nothing anybody could do – and all the time he was bleeding out, Fat Stan was standing on the promenade, just twenty yards away, gazing off in the direction of the Sands, as if he was deciding whether to head for home, or whether to go out for one last spot of night-hunting among the sandpipers and the black-tailed godwit.

The papers did a bit of a splash on knife crime, as if that was anything new, and the prosecution said Stan was nothing better than a common thug who had callously murdered Eddie Mac in a dispute over drugs – which was sort of true, but it didn't take into account the fact that Stan did what he did because he had no choice. He knew Eddie was after him and he was scared of getting done like that, getting a kicking in some back alley or out on the car park by the Sands – and I don't know why he didn't even try to explain that at the trial, just for the record. He didn't, though. He didn't say a word. Other than trying to get off with manslaughter, which was probably his lawyer's idea, he didn't do or say anything to help himself. I went to the trial every day and he didn't do anything but sit in the dock watching the judge, observing his movements and the way he carried himself, like he was observing one of those rare birds out on the Sands. Then, when they found him guilty of murder, he just stood up and went out and that was that. He didn't look at me, though he knew I was there. He didn't look at anybody. He was already gone in his own head, I think. He didn't belong in this world any more, he was already somewhere else and, even before the verdict was announced, he knew he was absent from the world that other people lived in, and it was weird, because I could see, as he walked out, eyes front, not saying a word, that it was like he'd been given an unexpected gift, an unexpected, terrible privilege that nobody could have foreseen – though now that it was there, it was as if it had been unavoidable all along. He had been touched by something, was how it looked to me. He had been touched and now he was steeped in a new gravity that nobody else could share or understand. It was like he was innocent, then, even though everybody knew he was guilty, and this innocence that he couldn't explain was his special secret, a secret that nobody else could know.

I didn't see him again, after that. When I left the court building, I went straight to the Raven and spent all the money I had on snakebite, then I went home and sat in my dad's shed, staring up at the moon through the open door till I drifted off. When I woke, I felt dirty and cold, but I didn't want to go inside, so I walked out to the Sands on my own. It was thick fog by the time I got there, thick, cold fog all the way from the car park to the water, and I stood awhile gazing out into that emptiness before I started walking, slow and careful, towards the faraway silvery line where the birds might be. You never knew exactly, though, and I must have strayed at some point on the walk out, because I never did get to the water and I didn't see any birds either. All I saw was whiteness. It was cold and the fog got thicker the further I went, and I kept thinking something would happen – I didn't know what, but I know I was waiting for something as I walked out across the Sands towards the place where the godwit lived. A ghostly figure at the tide line, a patch of nothingness where a person could fritter away in a matter of seconds, or maybe the hint of a body moving towards me through the fog like a hunter – I didn't know what I was expecting, but whatever it was, it didn't come and eventually I turned around and started following my own trail back to dry land, until my footprints disappeared and I was walking blindly over unmarked sand, heading by guesswork and instinct towards the place that I had started from, not really caring whether I was right or wrong, just aware of my weight and the uncertainty of the ground beneath my feet until, with a sudden, hard rush of relief and disappointment, I found the first sparse line of dune-grass and dry land.

THE BELL-RINGER

Half a mile beyond the sign for Lathockar mill, Eva Lowe turned off the main coastal road and took the back way through Kinaldy woods. It wasn't the most direct route into the village, but her father had always liked that stretch of road, maybe because it reminded him of Slovakia, and they'd often come this way on their Sunday walks, when her mother was still alive. It was dark, out on the narrow lane that ran past the sawmills; dark, and very green, the boundary wall a dim colony of moss and ferns, the shadows under the trees forever damp and still. To most people, it just seemed gloomy, but for Eva it was as close to the landscape of home as she could imagine – especially now, with new snow settling on the pines and on the ridges of the dry-stone wall, so that the land resembled nothing so much as the middle ground in some children's book illustration, the snow steady and insistent in a world that continued regardless, even when the entire kingdom succumbed to the bad fairy's spell and slept for a hundred years in a viridian web of gossamer and thorns. Her father had always loved that story, and she still had the book somewhere, her one real memento of him those water-colour drawings from a world that, even before she opened the book for the first time, was already gone forever, leaf-green and sky-blue and damson, cancelled out in a tide of cattle-trucks and unmarked graves.

Her father had been a long time dying, and Matt had lost patience with it all. He would never say what he was thinking, but it was clear that he resented the time she spent at the hospital and Eva had started looking forward to the days or weeks when her husband was away, inspecting a rig in the North Sea, or designing some mysterious installation in Egypt or Nigeria. During that last month, he'd been away more often than not, and that had been fine with Eva. It gave her a space to come to terms with things, a silence in which to remember her father's voice, singing to her in the language of his childhood, or reciting those old folk stories that he loved. Later, though, when it was all over, she found herself with nowhere to go and nothing to do, and nobody to talk to but Matt's sister, Martha, who had suddenly started coming to the house on Saturday mornings with cakes and baskets of apples. She never came when Matt was there, but when he was away she would invite herself over for coffee and a chat. It had become a fixture: a tradition, even; on Saturdays, around ten-thirty, Martha would arrive and they would sit by the Aga and have long conversations. Sometimes *too* long. It was Martha's fault, in fact, that she was late now, though Eva didn't mind that so much: her sister-in-law had been a good friend in those first days, when her grief was still raw. That was how Martha talked about such things, her language straight out of self-help books and women's magazines, but it had worked, at least in the beginning, and Eva had looked forward to those Saturday mornings, when they sat for hours over a plate of biscuits and told each other the stories people tell when they are trying to remember what it was they were doing before their lives were so rudely interrupted.

Looking back, though, Eva could see that the real interruption had not been her father's death. She had always known he would die, and she had tried to prepare herself for the loss. Of course, as Martha said, you can never be truly prepared for the death of a loved one, especially when it happens so slowly and painfully. Still, the fact was that, in the aftermath of the funeral, when it seemed as if the whole world had fallen silent, it was her marriage, not her father's absence, that troubled Eva most. Matt had come back for a few days to help with the arrangements, and she couldn't help but notice his relief that this phase of their existence was over, just as he seemed relieved to be going back to work once the business of the interment was over. Until then, she had thought it was her husband she was missing when she sat up at night staring out at the orchard and the fields beyond, fields that had once belonged to Matt's people and were now rented out to neighbours. Sometimes, she remembered him as he was when they had first met: his charm, his quiet sense of humour, the little games he played to amuse her, or to let her know what he couldn't say because – as he did say, often – he wasn't much for talking. She remembered how he would bring her flowers, or fruit from the orchard, and she remembered how, when it became clear that they were serious about one another, he had created that long-running joke about their having identical tattoos: hearts, roses, Celtic knots, tiny bluebirds tucked away in the secret angles of their bodies, where only they could see. That romantic phase hadn't lasted past the first year of marriage, but she still remembered it, if not in absolute detail, then at least as a story she could tell herself. When he'd first started travelling away, she had rehearsed it dutifully in her mind, because surely they had loved each other back then, and if they had loved each other once, then they could love each other again. Yet all the time she was aware of how deliberate that remembering was, and she knew, when she was alone, that it wasn't really Matt she was missing. She just didn't want to be alone.

No: the truth was, she didn't mind being on her own, it was just that she didn't like being alone in *that house*. If they had lived somewhere else, if Matt had sold up and bought a property in the village – a notion he'd brought up himself and considered for a long time before abandoning the idea – she would have been fine. She could have got by, even when he was away for months, living his separate life, not even bothering to phone for days on end and, when he did, making it clear that he had other things to think about, that this was just some duty he felt he had to perform, so Eva would know that they were all right. After they had finished those conversations about nothing, she would put down the phone and picture him in some bright room – a conference centre, perhaps, or a restaurant – discussing weighty business with colleagues, talking about engineering or politics just loud enough so the waitress would hear. Maybe he would flirt a little, and maybe he would do more. She could see him telling his little jokes, she could see how charming he would seem to the girl, who would be young and bright and eager to please. At such times, the house would close in around her, dark, damp, utterly still and yet, at the same time, busy with the echoes and memories of those who had gone before, generation upon generation of Lowes, all dark-eyed and stocky and taciturn, watching her from the shadows, listening when she spoke on the phone or on the odd occasion when she talked to herself, just to break the silence: listening, watching, judging. Sometimes she even imagined she saw them, though it was never final, never anything as conclusive as a haunting, just phantoms from the stories Matt had told her during the first days of their courting: Old John Lowe with his hurricane lamp coming in from the orchard; the twins, Maybeth and Cathy, sitting on the cold flagstones in the scullery amidst a litter of kittens; the stricken, defiantly cheerful Eleanor, laid out in what was now the guest room, dying slowly in her mid-teens, forty years before. Whenever Eva was alone in the house, they would make themselves known, not quite present, but there all the same, and it always seemed to her that they were waiting for something. After a while, she'd find herself talking, not so much to herself, as to them, pretending she was somebody else, trying to win them over, and she knew she had to get out. That house was driving her insane, and there was nobody she could talk to about it because, if she had said as much, people would have known for sure that she really was mad.

She hadn't known what to do at first; then, one afternoon when she had finished the shopping, she stayed on in the village, wandering about like a tourist, taking it all in. The church, the two pubs, the school. The large, well-kept green, with its row of chestnut trees on the south side. This was her home, but she had to remind herself of the fact, and she didn't feel, as she wandered along the high street, that she was *known* here, she didn't really feel like a local. Her father had come to the place as a young man; she herself had gone to this very school, and her mother had stood in the queue at the butcher's with all the other women, picking out cuts of meat at one counter, then going over to the little kiosk at the back to pay. In those days, the people who prepared the meat didn't handle money, and she had liked that, the way they kept it all separate. The butcher had been a good man, friendly to her mother, always offering a kind word and picking her out the best cuts, but the wife had been mean and silent as she took the money, and sometimes she had kept it a little longer in her hand, staring at it, as if she thought it might not be proper currency. Those people were gone now, and the man who served the chops and sausages happily took her card without a second glance. Eva supposed it didn't matter now, but she missed the old ways.

At four o'clock, the church clock chimed, and she was about to go back to the car when she thought of the community centre. There was a café there, and she remembered that they had activities, flower arranging and Italian classes, Toc-H, the Women's Institute. She didn't see herself as the WI type, and she wasn't even sure what Toc-H was, but she had wandered over there anyhow, and she had located the noticeboards in the foyer, with the timetables for events and classes neatly pinned out in rows among notices for Brownies and photographs of children in karate whites. They had day classes and evening classes, mostly in the hall or the gym. Eva had considered yoga, because she thought it would be relaxing, but she had quickly dismissed the image of herself in a leotard. On Wednesday nights they had a beginner's class in French, which she'd done in school but completely forgotten, and she had more or less decided that this was for her when she saw a small white postcard, set apart from the rest, announcing that the bell-ringing club was looking for new members. *Everyone welcome*, it said; *no experience needed.*

If someone had asked Eva Lowe to imagine a typical bell-ringer, she would have pictured some churchy spinster in a hand-knitted cardigan and brogues, or maybe a man in a tweed hat and one of those Army & Navy store sweaters that all the keen hikers wore when they climbed the Ben, but reading that notice, she had a sudden notion of herself in a bell tower, standing in a circle of like-minded souls, the kindly faces touched with a warm, coppery lamplight, the bells ringing out over the stillness of the churchyard as the people of the village settled to their dinners, or rose from their beds and made ready for Sunday Service. She wasn't a religious person, as such, but she had always liked the church for its own sake, especially when it was lit with candles on Christmas Eve, or brimming with sheaves of barley and ripe fruit at harvest time. As a child, she had sometimes walked around the little graveyard during lunch-break, when the other kids were playing, and she had made a point of reading all the names on the stones. Her father had told her off for that: God was a lie, he said, and heaven was a myth. Yet Eva thought this place had less to do with God and his angels than with an ordinary, and understandable desire to have things continue as they had always done. Easter, Harvest, Christmas, it all went round, forever and ever, and nothing could change that. It was a pagan desire, she thought, and it was a pagan place: a dark garden of yews and straggling roses and, at its centre, the stone church, with its altar and its font, and above it all, the bells, suspended in the chill air of the belfry, heavy and still, but waiting to be brought to life. It surprised her, all this *stuff* running through her head as she stood there, reading the postcard; she hadn't thought of it before, or at least not in so many words. Nevertheless, she was decided. She took out her shopping list and jotted down the relevant contact details.

It turned out that the organiser was someone she remembered from school and, though the woman seemed not to know Eva by name, she had been very kind, and the other bell-ringers had been gentle and considerate, always ready to help her out, never saying anything when she got things wrong. Of course, Matt had laughed when she told him. He'd come home three weeks after she started and, after listening to her talk about it for a couple of minutes, he'd just shaken his head in that whatever-will-she-come-up-with-next way he had.

'Well, I'm glad you've found something you like,' he said. 'To be honest, I think you're crackers, but if it keeps you happy—' He'd noticed that she was annoyed then, and he'd stopped talking, but he didn't try to undo the damage. He wasn't that interested, hadn't been in a long time. Whenever he was home, he would spend hours on the phone, or go out to the pub with his old crowd; then he would be off again. Eva hadn't expected him to understand, but she was still hurt that he could be so dismissive. Hurt, and then, when she talked to Martha about it, angry, because Martha had been angry and that had made Eva's anger seem more justified. Needless to say, Martha had been totally supportive about the bell-ringing: supportive, but also intelligent, not just understanding, in some general way, that Eva needed a hobby, but *getting it* – getting, without having to be told, the whole thing about the lighted church and the belfry and that magical resonance of the bells ringing out over the fields and the village green. But then, that was how Martha had been from the first: she had always got it, she had always understood. She had understood how Eva felt about the house and, even though she was just as proud of her family history as Matt was, she could see how all that Lowe mythology might make an outsider feel uncomfortable. Eva had been impressed by that and later, as they had got to know one another, she had been gladdened by the idea that someone she knew, a friend, almost a sister, was happy with her lot. It gave her hope, and there were times when she wanted to be like Martha, so independent, so understanding, so determined to be her own woman and do the right thing.

So it had come as a shock, that morning, when Martha had announced that she was more or less having an affair with someone she had met in the village. She hadn't intended the revelation to *be* shocking, of course, she'd even tried to make light of it as they sat in the kitchen over a glass of wine. Eva didn't normally drink in the daytime but, maybe because it was so close to Christmas, she had fetched a bottle of white wine out of the fridge, instead of doling out the usual coffee and biscuits, and Martha had opened up after her second glass, talking about how unhappy she was with James, and how tired she was of being taken for granted.

'I'll pretend to other people,' she had said. 'But I won't go on pretending to myself.' She wasn't terribly upset; she wasn't even that emotional. Most of the time, when people talked about their problems, they were working things out as they go along, trying out ideas, looking for the reaction that will confirm them in whatever decision they are hoping to reach – but Martha wasn't like that. She had thought it all through beforehand, and was now simply confirming what she had decided. 'A person can die from lack of . . .' She considered a moment.

Eva was worried, afraid she was about to hear something embarrassing, but she didn't say anything. She didn't want to interrupt.

'*Contact*,' Martha said at last, with grim satisfaction. She gave Eva a curious look, as if she wanted to ask her something, then she let it go. 'I'm not talking about sex here,' she said. 'Or not *just* sex. I'm talking about *contact*. A hug, a touch, that's all.' She thought for a moment; then she bowed her head and gave a soft laugh. 'All right,' she said, looking up. 'I am talking about sex.'

Eva laughed back, but she wasn't happy. 'But what about James?' she said.

Martha waved her hand. 'To hell with James,' she said. When she was annoyed she looked older, and not so attractive – something she obviously knew, because she bowed her head again and sat a moment, considering what she'd said. Then, after a moment of quiet, she spoke again, her head still bowed, so Eva couldn't see her face. 'It's not as if it's going anywhere,' she said. She looked up, and her face was calm again, composed. 'It's just one of those things,' she said. 'I didn't plan on it. It just happened.'

Eva didn't know what to say. She remembered Martha telling her once that James was constitutionally mean, and she wondered what he was doing now, and whether he suspected anything. He was a big man, with large hands and a cruel mouth: a man used to getting his own way, at any price. A man like Matt, in fact. Casual and charming, but careless of others, steeped in quiet judgements and long-term calculation, his life a fixed agenda that, no matter what happened, would continue on its set course, to whatever end that he had decided he deserved. The one advantage, with such men, the one thing you could count on was that everything they did was governed by reason. If James found out about the affair, he wouldn't go out with a kitchen knife looking for Martha and her lover, he would find much finer ways – legal ways – to make their lives miserable.

Martha smiled, but she was far away, lost in her own thoughts. 'It's not as if it's going to change anything,' she said, more to herself than to anyone else. It was a minute or so before she looked back to Eva. 'You only live once, right?' she said.

Eva shook her head and stood up. Suddenly, she had to *do* something, she had to get herself organised, clear away the glasses, get ready. She knew Martha would take it badly, but she needed to be out of the house, away from the ancestors in the walls, listening in to Martha's confession, away from the thought of Matt, and what he would think if he knew what his sister was up to. Worse, what he would do, if this affair continued and he discovered that Eva had known about it from the start. She picked up the wine bottle and carried it over to the sink. 'My God, look at the time,' she said, aware of how awkward this diversion was, of how inconsiderate she was being. She turned and gave Martha a quick glance. She felt guilty, but she was annoyed too, annoyed and resentful, because she didn't want this secret – or maybe it was because she didn't want to have to think about all this, about contact and affairs and things that just happen.

Martha looked more surprised than upset. Surprised – and a little confused from the wine, probably. 'Is there somewhere you have to be?' she asked.

Eva stopped making herself busy and looked her in the face. 'I'm sorry,' she said. 'I just . . .' She considered for a moment, then she looked away quickly, blinking back tears that she hadn't expected – and the fact that she was about to cry was somehow the worst of it all, something grotesque and foolish, a self-imposed humiliation.

Martha's expression didn't change; she still seemed surprised, rather than offended or upset and, if anything, she appeared to be more concerned for Eva than with her own problems. 'I'm sorry,' she said. 'I shouldn't have told you about it.' She looked at her glass and saw that it was almost empty. She sat back, and smiled ruefully. 'Some secrets are better kept secret,' she said.

Eva shook her head. 'It's not that,' she said. 'I hope you'll be – happy.' She sat down and tried to collect her thoughts. She wanted to be gone, to be in the church, with the bells ringing in her head.

Martha laughed. 'Well, I doubt that,' she said, with just the hint of a hard edge in her voice. She gave Eva a long look, then she shook her head and laughed again. 'I doubt anybody will come out of this *happy*,' she said.

Eva was angry now. She didn't understand, or maybe she did, but if she did, she didn't want to, and she didn't see the point of breaking things for no reason. Before she could think better of it, she had spoken and, though she didn't mean it to sound dismissive, she wasn't sorry when it did. 'Well, there you go,' she said.

Martha froze for a moment and stared at her. Then she laughed again and raised her glass. 'There you go,' she said, without a trace of mockery or dismissal. 'There you go, indeed.' She tossed back what little remained of the wine. 'And God Bless Us, One and All,' she said, as she rose, fetched her coat from the hat stand and made herself ready to go.

When Eva arrived at the church, the others were already there, but she wasn't late. Nobody said much, but then they never did: by now, she knew these people, but she didn't know their lives, or their inner thoughts, she only ever saw them in this place, when they were doing the thing they loved most, a group of like-minded souls, equals in discretion, united by a common tact. Nobody here was about to pry, or break the unspoken rule that said, without ever needing to be stated in so many words, that they were all here for one reason, and for one reason only. The world outside and what they did there was another matter altogether. Nobody cared what you were in that outside world, nobody enquired about family or work, everyone just got on with it. Eva knew them all by name, of course, and some of the faces were semi-familiar, but when they were here, gathered in a circle beneath the bells, it didn't really matter who they were. Richard, Catherine, Grace, Simon, John – she knew them all for an hour and a half on a Saturday afternoon, but as soon as they put on their coats and scarves and – yes, it so happened that some of them, at least, fitted the image she'd had of them that first day – their tweed caps and bicycle clips, they seemed to dwindle away, the light going out of their faces, secret selves discarded for their return to the outside world. It had come as a surprise to her, those first few weeks: the reason she had joined the group originally had been to make new friends, but now she was grateful for the fact that nobody here wanted to do anything but gather at the appointed time, ring the bells, and go home.

The only exception to all this was Harley. He was the newest member of the group, and he was nothing like the others. He'd been something of a surprise, to be honest: young, casually dressed and very good-looking, he was an American student from Illinois, or Iowa, or some such place. No doubt, he had come along the first time out of curiosity, because bell-ringing struck him as quaint and Olde Worlde, like warm beer or clootie dumpling, and so one of the experiences it would be a shame to miss while he was over here. He'd taken to it, though, and the group had accommodated him easily, in spite of his youth and his accent and his fondness for sweatshirts with oddly unsettling slogans printed across the front. Catherine was particularly considerate of him, bringing in brown paper bags full of apples from her garden and Tupperware containers of mince pies to share with his housemates. She was old enough to be his mother, but Eva wasn't so sure her attentions were wholly maternal. Of course, Harley was always polite with her, in the way that Americans are: doggedly courteous and, at the same time, utterly remote, like the landing party in an old episode of *Star Trek*, curious and well-meaning and occasionally bewildered, but sworn not to interfere in the everyday life of their hosts.

For her own part, Eva was as scrupulously polite with Harley as he was with her − and just as distant. Yet there were times when she imagined − not sex, of course, nothing so vivid − but a shared moment of some kind. A picnic, say, on Balcomie Law, or a long walk in the woods by Lathockar, where she would listen to his stories about Illinois, or Iowa, or wherever he was from. In these imaginings, they never touched − not because Harley didn't excite her, but because she'd suddenly discovered that she was superstitious, and she was afraid to imagine what she most desired, afraid even to wonder what it might be because, as soon as she did, as soon as she pictured it, or put it into words, it would fall away into the dark, cold realm of the impossible. That afternoon, however, she couldn't help thinking about what Martha had said and, as Harley moved back and forth in the dim space of the bell tower, she'd noticed how beautiful his hands were: fine, almost delicate, not large and heavy, like the other men she knew, but strong nevertheless, like a pianist's hands, or a dancer's. Of course, as soon as the notion entered her mind, she did everything she could to nip it in the bud, because she didn't want to think about him, or not in that way. Yet no matter what she did, she kept coming back to him: to his dark eyes, to the way he carried himself and, time and again, before she could stop herself, to the beauty of his hands. Hands she wanted to feel on her skin, light and slow and graceful; not heavy, never heavy, but gentle the way a bird is when it alights on a branch or a stone, resting for a moment, but never entirely settled, always light, always about to take off at any moment.

And all this time, as she thought about Harley, the bells rang out over the snowy land. It had surprised Eva, during those first few weeks, that her hobby came to matter so much to her. She had come with the intention of making new friends, but she had ended up falling in love with the sound of the bells, by the sounds she made and the sounds they made together, she and the others in their little group, she and the others and Harley, with his light, strong hands. Together, they were continuing a tradition that had once been central to the life of the entire community, and she liked to think that, only a generation ago, whenever these bells had rung out over the fields and the streets, everyone had known what they were saying. A call to worship; a royal wedding; an armistice; an enemy attack. Everyone would have understood those signals, because those were the public events, those were the facts. Yet surely there had been something else, another music inside the public proclamations, and there must have been those who could hear more than the facts, gifted listeners who could pick out the subtleties in the way one bell worked against the others, say, or in the pauses when one ringer stopped, weary or undecided, or touched with the knowledge of imminent mortality. Now, the bells were nothing but background – pure atmosphere, a little local colour – but perhaps there were still souls in this very parish who could decipher the inner workings of a bell-ringer's mind, or of her heart, just by listening. If such souls existed, they might know everything about her: the lie of her marriage, her secret thoughts about Harley, her half-formed plans to get away. With every pull on the bell rope, she might be confiding everything to some old man in the almshouses at the far end of the village, or some dying woman in one of the cottages out by the woods, some seasoned listener who would set aside a book or a pile of darning and listen awhile, wondering who it was they were hearing, wondering who it was that was giving herself away. It frightened her, that notion, but it pleased her too, because she wanted to proclaim the truth, she wanted to ring out who she really was, how she wasn't the good and faithful wife she pretended to be, but someone else, someone interrupted. That was what she wanted to say – not to confess, but to proclaim to all the land – and that was what she did proclaim, to whoever might be listening, and if there was nobody, then even that was better than nothing. Yet there *had* to be someone and, all that afternoon, as she stood in that company of bells, she wondered what that privileged listener might be hearing, in the bells and in the silence that came after, when practice was over, and they all went back to their separate lives.

It was snowing again. Over the green, the lights had come on in the shops, the usual gold and white mixed with the Christmas decorations, red and green and a pale, otherworldly blue around the doors and windows of the butcher's and the greengrocer's. Eva was dreading Christmas now: James and Martha would come over as usual, and she would have to sit in that house with them, pretending everything was normal, drinking sherry while the men talked, passing round the mince pies and trying not to be offended by Matt's jokes about her baking. This year, she decided, she would buy mince pies from the new delicatessen, the one that sold Polish sausage and French cheese, just to see if anybody noticed the difference. Better still, she would just disappear, maybe go out for a walk in the woods by herself, in the white and the quiet. She would leave a trail of footprints in the snow and, when she got to the end of the track, she would look back, the way her father had always done on their winter walks, when she was a girl and her mother was not long dead – and it struck her that she'd never really allowed herself time to go back to the woods, or out to the meadows where her father had sometimes led her, in the dusk of a summer's evening, to look at the moths, naming them, first in the language he had been obliged to learn as a young man, the only language Eva knew, and then in his mother tongue, being careful to match the two, even though the moths they found, ash-grey and soft on the barks of the trees and the stones, were local to this place and only distantly related to those he had known as a boy.

'You OK?'

Eva turned and saw Harley in the shelter of the porch behind her, his coat buttoned up to the neck, a thick woollen crew-cap pulled down over his ears. She remembered that he'd told her once that he was accustomed to cold weather, where he was from. Illinois, she thought, though it might have been Iowa – she wished she could remember which, and she wished she knew what kind of country it was, whether it was prairie, or forest, or just mile after mile of suburb or strip mall, like the America on television crime shows. She nodded. 'I was just thinking we'd get a white Christmas this year,' she said. 'But then, I suppose you're used to that, where you live.'

He grinned. 'Oh, we get plenty of snow, all right,' he said. 'Masses of it.' He paused for a moment, considering, and Eva thought she saw something in his face: a memory, or maybe a trace of homesickness. It made him seem faraway and dark, whatever it was, or maybe just preoccupied, like someone who knows he has lost something and can't for the moment remember what it is. Maybe it was a girl. There would be a girl, of course; a pretty girl in Illinois, or Iowa, a girl with long dark hair and reading glasses that she only wore when she wanted to look serious. A pretty girl, and not just pretty but smart. Pretty and smart, and funny, too. A smart, funny girl who talked more than he did, which was why he loved her, or maybe why she loved him.

'Will you be going home for Christmas?' she asked.

He looked puzzled, as if her question had been terribly personal and inappropriate, then his face brightened. 'Oh, no,' he said. 'I'm planning to travel around, maybe go to Paris.'

'Paris?' For some reason, the idea shocked her. 'For Christmas?'

He laughed. 'I don't know,' he said. 'Maybe Paris, maybe somewhere else.' He poked his head out from under the shelter of the porch and looked up into the falling snow. 'Maybe I'll just stay here,' he said.

Eva shook her head. 'Oh, don't do that,' she said. 'Go to Paris. Go skiing or something, but don't stay here.'

Harley laughed again, then he saw how serious she looked and he nodded. Eva tried to smile then, because she knew she had given something away, but she couldn't, because she suddenly felt sorry for him, and for the pretty, smart girl in Iowa, with her books and her reading glasses. She knew how ridiculous that was, and she wanted to shrug it off, to stop being such a fool – and maybe Harley sensed that, because he touched her, just for a moment, his hand alighting on her coat sleeve and lingering for a moment, before he took it away. 'I have to go,' he said. 'Have a nice evening, OK?'

Eva nodded, and this time she did smile, but Harley was already moving away, loping off towards the gate in his winter coat, the snow clinging to his coat sleeves and the wool cap as he stepped out on to the pavement and headed across the green. Eva knew that she should go too, but she couldn't bring herself to go back to the car and drive home to her husband's house, and she lingered in the porch awhile, watching the snow as it fell through the shop lights on the far side of the green. Harley was gone: he had vanished suddenly and she was surprised, because he'd been there a moment before, crossing the green, heading towards the row of shops opposite. She didn't know where he lived, but she knew it was in a shared house somewhere outside the village, probably on the west side, out by the woods. It would be a half-mile or so, maybe more, and the thought struck her that she should have thought to offer him a lift, because he didn't have a car, and he'd get cold walking back to wherever he stayed, even with the coat and hat. But then, he was used to the cold and, besides, it would have been dangerous to get into a car with him and drive up through the Kinaldy woods in the snow. Out there alone with him, in the dark, with snow falling all around them, she might have said something she would have regretted, and he would have felt bad for her – and at that moment, Harley feeling bad for her was the one thing Eva couldn't bear.

But then, he hadn't appeared on the far side of the green, and she'd wondered where he'd gone, not because she wanted to give in to the temptation to catch him up and drive him home to his warm house, but out of simple curiosity. That was what made her step out into the snow and walk out to the gate – because she just couldn't figure out where he had gone. It was like when you watch a conjuror perform a magic trick, and you shouldn't really care, because you know it's an illusion, but you just have to try and figure out how it's done. Only she couldn't figure it out, because Harley wasn't there. He was gone. The others were gone too, all but Catherine, who was putting something into the boot of her car twenty yards further along, and there was nobody in the shops opposite, or nobody but the ones who served there – the girl in the greengrocer's, come round from behind the counter to stare out at the falling snow, the butcher in his white coat, clearing away the slabs of beef and lamb after a busy day. Eva felt cheated, as if Harley had tricked her on purpose – and for a moment the thought scared her, because if he had, he would have done it for a reason, and what other reason could there be than that he knew how she felt about him, and was mocking her. But then, maybe he'd *wanted* her to look for him, maybe he'd wanted that lift, but couldn't ask, because she was a married woman and he was an outsider. That was ridiculous, of course, but it was just as ridiculous that he would go to all this trouble to make fun of her. The sad truth, surely, was that he'd already forgotten she even existed, and was already on his way home, trudging happily through the snow: a young man, used to the cold, heading for home in a place he would never see again. Surely that was it, Eva told herself – yet she looked for him still, and she still expected to see him, coming back to resume the conversation, because he had seen something in her face, something he'd looked for all along, but hadn't expected. She stood at the gate, snow lining the creases in her coat, her face and hands already numb with cold, and she waited to see what would happen, because something would happen, she knew it would. And just as that thought came to her, as if on cue, a familiar car appeared on the far side of the green. It was moving slowly, and the driver's-side window was wound down, so Eva could see that it was Martha, her hair damp from the drifting snow, her face attentive, as she gazed across the green towards the trees by the church. For a moment, Eva was annoyed. She thought Martha had come for her and, even though it made no sense, even though she didn't want to be drawn back into that morning's conversation, she lifted her hand, lifted it without thinking, and waved. She waved, and then she waved again – but Martha didn't see her, and at that same moment, a few yards off to the left, a dark figure detached itself from the shadow of the big chestnut tree and hurried across, a dark figure that Eva knew from somewhere, though at first she couldn't place it, because it didn't make any sense: a dark figure who, after a moment, became

Harley, running around the car and getting in on the passenger side with an air of having done this before. As soon as he was in, the car pulled away, heading out of the village and west, towards the lower woods, where the snow would be thick all night, thick and heavy and, even on the road that ran up to Kinaldy and Lathockar, completely unmarked, except for a line of tyre tracks that would soon vanish into whiteness.

THE DEER LARDER

The first email arrived on a Thursday evening, around nine o'clock. I remember it quite clearly, because I had spent the day at the hospital, going from one department to the next, having various tests and X-rays done before ending up back in rheumatology, being examined by my usual doctor and a very tall, rather pretty student who hadn't quite mastered the necessary air of professional detachment. The consultant was detached enough for them both, though. As usual. Which is not to say that she was lacking in any way – quite the contrary, in fact. No: as always, Elizabeth Marsh – my beautiful, shrewd, faintly glamorous doctor – displayed the reassuring mix of good humour, consideration and mild irony that made me thankful I had been assigned to a female specialist rather than a man. If there is one thing that I cannot abide, it's the seriousness of male professionals.

Still, St Hubert's was a teaching hospital so, with the best will in the world, it was hard not to feel like the Elephant Man as she pointed out the various interesting features of my disease: the localised but fairly extreme psoriasis, the odd little pools of inflammation on the scan, the visibly damaged areas revealed by the X-rays, while the younger woman – whose dark hair and very blue eyes reminded me, each time our eyes met, of a girlfriend I'd had twenty years before – tried to seem unperturbed. Of course, I knew things had worsened since my last appointment, but I had tried not to think about it too much. Some of the pain was new, but I'm a fairly old hand at this by now and I've been preparing myself for this slow fall into creaky middle age since my first bout of iritis back in the early 90s. I do my bit to keep the whole process civilised: I take an interest, I make light, I use the kind of language doctors like – which is to say, accurate and undramatic, the language of a detached observer, descriptive, neutral and, most important of all, entirely innocent of any pretence to clinical knowledge. Privately, I am fascinated by the way it all works – the body, the disease, the cause and effect, the observable phenomena, the management of pain and expectations. Still, I'm always glad to get back home and be alone again – and that night was no different. Few pleasures equal the relief that comes from locking the front door behind me, turning on the desk lamp and settling down to work. The relief, and the simple happiness.

The email arrived just as I was taking my first break. My routine is pretty consistent: I do a few pages – I write commercial film scripts, mostly for training and PR companies – then I get a pot of coffee going and check my emails. That night, it was the only item in my inbox, which was odd, because there are usually masses of minor tasks and requests to deal with. At first sight, I thought it was one of those joke mails that sometimes slip through the spam detector, a specimen of those random fragments of surreal narrative that people send out by the thousand to complete strangers – presumably for some reason known to them, though I have never been able to figure out what that reason might be. My ISP is pretty good at filtering out that kind of thing, but occasionally they get through – sad little narratives of trouble and desire, of achievement and loss, always starting in the middle of the story and never reaching anything so satisfying as an end. This seemed no different, in spite of the fact that it was addressed to a specific individual, someone the sender seemed to know fairly well. But then, that might have been part of the game, part of the art, as it were.

On the other hand, this email might have ended up in my inbox because of a simple error – an address badly transcribed or mistyped after a long day's work, or a few too many glasses of wine. For some reason, I didn't delete the message right away, so I can quote it in full:

Dear Monique

Well, here I am on the island, sitting in my little study with a nice glass of – guess what? – and hammering away at the Maupassant book. Finally. Got heaps done already and I've only been here four days. I've got to 'La Maison Tellier' and I still can't get over how wonderful it is – how wonderful, and how terrifying when you think of what's to come and how this book foreshadows it all.

It's beautiful here, on this side of the island. This morning started out grey and drizzly, but by mid-afternoon it had cleared and now, in this soft, slightly pastel early evening light, it's completely still, the kind of stillness where everything seems more vivid and, at the same time, more convincing. From the window, all I can see is the flat expanse of the water, still as mercury, and the white hull of a sailing boat, moored just opposite the jetty by our one and only shop. It's preternaturally serene, utterly calm and almost silent – yet it's changing all the time. Something is always shifting. The light, the colours, the reflections. In the evenings, the water can be periwinkle blue for half an hour or so before it darkens, smooth, though not in a hard way, but with a strange surface tension, a strange perturbability to it. Like quicksilver – yes, like quicksilver, always about to change, always on the point of shifting and, at the same time, so very smooth, so very still.

You would love it here. And I meant what I said in my last email – you really are welcome any time. It's easy enough to get here – just let me know and I'll pick you up at the ferry. I promise I won't make a big thing of it, and I'm not asking you to change your mind. Honestly. I just think it's silly for us not to be friends, don't you think?

Love
Martin

That was all. It wasn't particularly interesting, it was even slightly embarrassing, to have been given such an unexpected glimpse of Martin's sad love life. Obviously, Monique had recently dumped him, probably for someone a little less wet and, despite those assurances to the contrary, his rhapsodies about the island were intended to get her back, on any terms, if only for a few intense and awkward days. Then, of course, the arguments would begin again – I knew that scenario well enough, after all – and there would be tears, *his* probably, before the week was out. No: there was nothing very interesting about this little love story and, to be honest, the only thing that caught my attention was the mention of Maupassant. It wasn't six months since I had written a script, for an educational production company, about Maupassant and Poe, and I'd been captivated by the beauty of the man's work – a beauty that seemed to me unbearably poignant, considering how painful and squalid the life had been. Of course, if I'd been more attentive that first night, I would have seen the reference to Maupassant – the mad syphilitic who wrote one or two of the most horrifying stories in the entire European tradition – as an obvious clue, a pointer to the game that was about to be played. And for as long as I could manage it, I convinced myself that what happened next really was a game, a diversion, like so many other diversions that one finds out there in the cold reaches of cyberspace, where nothing is as it seems and everything, from the latest atrocities in Gaza or Chad to the antics of *Big Brother*, has the quality and status of a diversion.

But I wasn't paying attention – on the contrary. I was thinking about the side effects of the new drugs I had just been prescribed, about my diminishing skills as a touch-typist – my fingers had already started to warp into strange shapes over the keyboard – and, most of all, I was thinking about happiness, and about how much time remained before the solitude I had worked so hard to attain was transformed from a joy into a burden by the vagaries of my far from rare disease.

For the next several days, I had no commitments – which meant I could stay in the flat and work as and when I liked, breaking off for coffee and a tuna sandwich, or an old movie on DVD, before returning to my desk for one of those small revelations that makes everything magical. When I say *small* revelations, I'm not being overly modest: I don't entertain big ideas, not these days anyway, and I have no illusions about my supposed talents. I just take what somebody else gives me – a defined project, with clear limits and constraints – and I try to light it up, somehow, like a medieval copyist illuminating his given text. Maybe I wanted something else when I first started out, but nowadays, this is enough. I work according to my own schedule and, occasionally, I create something that shines – shines, yes, even if it's only for a few moments in a mostly workaday piece. This is as much as I am allowed by the job I have chosen to do, but it turns out to be more than enough and, even now, when my body has started to betray me in all manner of subtle, yet utterly persuasive ways, I can still be surprised by the happiness I feel when I lock myself away and get to work, knowing that I won't be interrupted. Sometimes I want to kick myself for not having arrived at this place sooner – because it took me a ridiculously long time to realise that happiness was a much simpler proposition than I had first imagined. Growing up, we think it's going to be some big event: love at first sight, say, or a brilliant career; glittering prizes; a perfect wife; beautiful, gifted children. I have none of these things, but I am comfortable and I do work that, more often than not, I enjoy, work that leaves room in my day-to-day existence for the unglamorous, apparently negligible events that, cumulatively, add up to a more or less happy life. That's why there are no novels, or plays, or Hollywood movies about happiness. It's too ordinary, and it's too slow.

The second email, followed almost immediately by the third, came three days after the first and, together, they betrayed a change of mood. That didn't surprise me – it would have been foolish of Monique to accept Martin's invitation, or even to take it seriously – but I was a little annoyed that the mistake, if it was a mistake, had been repeated. I was also somewhat embarrassed by the tone of the messages – there was an ugly desperation to them that made me a little queasy – and I deleted them immediately. I guessed that Martin had been drunk when he wrote them and I was fairly certain that he would wake the next morning feeling more than a little shamefaced. I even expected to receive an apology, sooner rather than later – and I was surprised again when it didn't come the very next day.

The one thing that didn't occur to me was to reply to Martin and inform him of his mistake – and, looking back, I don't know why I didn't do exactly that. Maybe I was embarrassed for myself, as well as for him. Maybe it was all too close to the bone, too much of a reminder of my own lover's folly. I didn't need any reminder of the old days – of the lovely and self-deceived time before I came to understand that wonderful remark of Maurois (a man who knew a thing or two about romantic love), a remark that has been taped to the wall next to my computer for years now:

LE BONHEUR EST UNE FLEUR QU'IL NE FAUT PAS CUEILLIR

I think, at the time, I even considered emailing those words to my mysterious correspondent, with a simple explanation of what had happened – but I didn't. If I had, I could have put this matter by and forgotten it – a choice that, for the basest of reasons, was no longer possible after the fourth email arrived, two days later, on a clear green evening when the city was winding up the business of the day and switching its lights on, one by one, silver and cherry-red and gold, for the night to come.

It began abruptly: no greeting, no reference to the earlier emails, no attempt at a preamble. It assumed something it had no business to assume – or so it seemed until it occurred to me again that this was a piece of artifice, a device to draw me into the story. Or not me, exactly – I was quite certain that I had not been targeted, as such – but the reader. Because, surely this was a fiction. Surely this was a literary game, a diversion that someone out there had devised for his own reasons – Martin, not Martin, it hardly mattered. Anybody can be anybody in cyberspace, after all – a fact that, on reflection, seems to me quite appalling now. It's all flimflam; it's all a con. I've always disliked the telephone because I can't see the other person's face – yet for years I was happy to conduct my business almost entirely by email, where I couldn't even hear a voice, or know if it was a man or a woman, a friend or a foe, even a person or a program that I was dealing with.

I'm not sure how to tell this, the email began. You're going to think I'm crazy, or maybe you'll just put it down to too little sleep and my usual overactive imagination – and it's true, I haven't been sleeping, I've hardly slept at all since I got here in fact, but what I am about to tell you isn't some hallucination and it certainly didn't spring from my overtired or overactive mind. In fact, it didn't come from anywhere. It was just – there. It's been there all along; I just didn't see it till now.

If you remember, I said I was going to go for a long walk to clear my head

– I didn't remember this, of course, because he hadn't said
anything of the kind –

*and that's where I was today, all day, walking on the old
trail that runs clear across the island, up through the hills
and over to the west side. The trail was made by some old
one-legged patriarch from the late nineteenth century – he'd
ride back and forth with his retinue all around him, surveying
his domain, or stalking the deer, or whatever it was they
did back then, and his people would keep it in order, all
eight or so miles of it, from the eastern shore to a high pass
through the hills and then down, past waterfalls and huge,
tumbled rocks to this beautiful, lonely beach on the western
side. On that side, there are no roads, so the only way to
get to that beach is on foot, via this old track, which is
mostly just a trail through the peat now, though there are
still places where you find stone walkways and sometimes
there will be an old culvert, with water running under your
feet, or you'll find a couple of stepping stones in a shallow
burn, buried in water that can be tobacco-dark with the
peat or cool and clear as the cream of the well. Only sometimes, though. The rest of the time – when the burn is deep,
say, or where the old track has crumbled away – it's all
about wading through waist-high water, or slopping across
wet peat and rushes or, worst of all, fighting your way
through chest-high bracken, not knowing what's in there
with you, waiting to strike at your ankles or leaping unno-
ticed into your clothes and hair. Midges, ticks, something
the local folk call keds – and who knows what else. Let's
just say it's no idyll. Still, for a while I was glad I'd made
the effort. It was good to be out in the air, good to be out
in the open, away from the house, with its frightful, yet
strangely appealing shadows.*

*Anyhow, I got across fine and I stood a long time on
the beach, communing with whatever was out there – I'm
not going to say Nature, because it wasn't that, or not in*

the usual sense. Of course, I thought of you, and I wished you were with me. I stood awhile and looked out across the water and thought my thoughts. Then, just as I started to think about heading back, it started to rain. Nothing much, at first, just a slow, sweet smirr, more mist than rain really. Scotch mist, or something like it. It wasn't that bad and, to be honest, the ground was so wet underfoot, the paths streaming with cold water and the peat so thick and spongy, it was barely a step up from bog, so a little bit more wet wasn't going to make that much of a difference.

Well, that's what I thought to begin with. By the time I got back up on to the hill, though, it was pouring down, thick, heavy rain bouncing off my face and hands – I'd not thought to bring gloves, and my hands were suddenly freezing – so I could hardly see where I was going. The only thing for it was to put my head down and plod on, following the path where it led and trusting that I wouldn't go astray – and, of course, that was exactly what I did. I had a map, but it was useless out there and, anyway, by the time I realised how far off-track I'd gone, it was sodden through. So I just kept going, trying to remember landmarks I had seen on my way over and keeping the big hill to my right. The fairy hill, they call it, but I don't think they're thinking about the fairies in children's books. I wasn't too worried, not to begin with at least. Mostly I was just annoyed with myself for not being better prepared. But I was OK, in spite of everything. I was trying to see it as an adventure, and I was thinking about getting back to the house and getting into a nice hot bath with a big tumbler of whisky and some music on the radio.

When I first caught sight of the girl, I didn't believe she was real. I thought it was a mirage, or maybe some kind of Brocken spectre, one of those tricks of the light or the gloaming that hill walkers tell you about. I mean, what else could I think? One moment, I was alone and then, suddenly, she was there, walking beside me, step for step, through the wet peat. She had her head down – she didn't look at me, not once – but she knew I was there. She knew I was there from the first – and that was why her head was down, because I was there. She didn't want to look at me, she was desperately trying to pretend I wasn't there – and it came to me, why I cannot begin to think, but it came to me that she was frightened. I frightened her. And, God knows, she frightened me too – but what frightened me most, at that moment, was her fear. Because, at that moment, as we walked in step through the driving rain, I felt like a monster, or an apparition. That's how I still feel, now that I'm back, and neither the bath nor the whisky – not one, but four, maybe five big glasses of the stuff – can change that fact.

I don't know how long she was there, beside me. It felt like ages, but it probably wasn't and then, just as suddenly as she had come, she was gone, and I was alone again, trudging home in the rain, though at that very moment when I noticed she wasn't with me any more, I saw something – a configuration of rocks, a dark, kidney-shaped lochan in the middle distance – that told me I wasn't far from the car park where I had started out that morning, and I pressed on, trying to tell myself that it had all been a trick of the weather, a hallucination and nothing more, born out of fatigue and confusion. An hour later, I was behind the wheel of the car: sodden, frozen, caked in mud and peat, but safe.

But here's the thing. I'm back, and I'm warm and I'm all alone behind a locked door – but I'm not safe at all, and I'm not alone, even if there's nobody here with me. And I know it sounds crazy, but I can't help thinking that something I should have left behind out there on the moor has come indoors and is hidden in the house somewhere, waiting to materialise. I'm not talking about a ghost, or some fairy creature from the old stories – I'm not even talking about that girl, I'm just – I don't know—

I know this sounds crazy, but please believe me when I say it's real. I'm not imagining it, it's here – it's here right now, somewhere at the edge of my vision, just outside the door or in a far corner of the house, and it's not something I can give a name to, but it's there and it has something to do with that girl. It's not like some ghost in a film, and it's not threatening or sinister, or not exactly. If anything, it's something more abstract than that, some disembodied current of fear or apprehension or

And that was where the message ended. In mid-sentence, just like that. Maybe he had hit the send button by accident, maybe he'd just given up trying to express what he couldn't put into words and, maybe, just maybe, something terrible had happened. Something that might bring Monique to his aid, and so begin the inevitable process of reconciliation. And then again, maybe – and as soon as the thought occurred to me, I was immediately certain that I had guessed the truth – maybe this was all part of the game: a cliffhanger in a to-be-continued serial novel, designed to keep me – Martin/Not-Martin's anonymous reader – in suspense till the next instalment arrived.

I thought again of the Maupassant reference in the first message, and I had to smile. It was, quite clearly, a literary divertissement, a modern-day Horla story for the virtual world – and where better to accommodate Maupassant's terrifying sliver of nothingness than in cyberspace – and no doubt it would run and run. And I have to admit, this thought came as something of a relief. I had started to dislike poor lovesick Martin in his island hideaway. He certainly struck me as someone who had no business writing a biography of Maupassant. In fact, the very idea offended me. Now that I knew he was only a character, a literary invention, I could relax. That's how it is when you have attained the fragile, or perhaps I should say provisional condition of happiness – there are so many minor events, so many possible defects to the texture of existence that place it in jeopardy. Considered in that light, it's not so hard to see why, having broken his finger, Diogenes committed suicide: a moment's happiness is enough, if it is held uncontaminated in the tide of events, but it has to be perfect. It has to be incorruptible.

I fully expected another email the next morning and I was surprised when nothing out of the ordinary showed up in my inbox. But then, I told myself, perhaps that was part of the game too. Perhaps my correspondent was savouring the fact that, as a storyteller, he had all the time in the world.

Whatever the reason, the next email didn't appear until four days had passed and, when it did, it was darker, and more conventional in approach. It even reminded me of those nineteenth-century stories I had read so closely when I'd worked on the Maupassant piece, beautiful, subtle stories where the first glimmers of existentialism began to shine through the fabric of the everyday – and I recalled the pleasure I had taken in that double nostalgia, first for the monochrome, coffee- and tobacco-scented nothingness-haunts-being mood of the 50s, and then, going back in time, for the damp, musty folds of bourgeois dread that prefigured it.

The email was four pages long: oddly formal, suffused with a sense of inevitable doom, it was more than a little overdone, but it had its moments, nevertheless. The best passage came when Martin – I saw him, now, as something of a dandy, a displaced *fin de siècle* poet sitting at a computer screen in an office somewhere, making up stories for an unknown reader in the off hours – described his second encounter with the girl he'd met on the moor:

You remember I told you about the odd little hut behind the house

– I didn't remember, of course, but that was of no consequence –

and how I couldn't figure out what it was. It turns out that it's a deer larder, which is to say, a place where they used to hang the carcasses of the deer when they brought them in off the moor. It's louvered all the way round, so the wind blows through the slats and dries the meat – I looked this up in a book, and it really is fascinating how it works, how the wind blows through and the meat dries slowly. They say it's much better than a cold store, but nobody's allowed to use them any more, because of health and safety regulations—

Anyway, the next morning after my walk on the moor, I had this sudden, almost frantic urge to see inside – only it was locked and it took me a long time to find the key. I had to search and search and then finally I found it in a drawer in the kitchen, under a pile of old rags. I don't know why it was so important to me, but it was – I had to see what it was like, I just had to.

Anyway, I finally unlocked the door and I stepped inside. Nobody had been in there for years, everything was covered in dust and cobwebs, and there wasn't much to see, just a few hooks hanging from a beam and a heap of old sacking. It had a dirt floor, and it smelled of earth and damp and, behind it all, a subtle trace of something in a far corner, something almost sweet, like iron, or rust. There was no light, of course, and even though it was only ten or twelve feet deep, I couldn't see into the far corner – or rather, I couldn't see clearly, though I could make out a shape, some solid object, maybe a table, set against the back wall and, on it, something that I couldn't see at all, probably just more sacking, or some other junk. There was no reason to investigate further – it was just an old shed, really – but I couldn't let it go, just like that. Something was there, and I had to know what it was.

I moved forward, slowly, careful of the dark, not at all sure what I expected to find, but I knew I would find something. About halfway across, as I came within reach of the table – and that was what it was, a long, narrow table, about three feet off the ground – I saw that what I had taken for a heap of rags was actually a body, not a deer, but a person and then, slowly, with a sudden sense of total horror, as if I had caught myself in the commission of some vicious and perverse crime, I saw that it was the girl, the one I had seen on the moor, and I realised that she was watching me – that she had, in fact, been watching me since I'd first entered the room. And, though she didn't say anything, though she didn't cry out or even move from where she was lying, I could see that she was terrified. I wanted to say something, I wanted to reassure her, but I knew it was hopeless. Anything I said would be a lie – I don't know how I knew this but I did, I knew it as surely as I have ever known anything – whatever I said would be a lie and I knew, immediately, that she was right to be afraid. Because I really was the monster she thought I was. I really was her worst nightmare, in the flesh—

The email broke off then, and the story wasn't taken up for several days. Of course, I thought this wasn't altogether fair and it annoyed me to think that, having got me hooked, my correspondent was growing tired of his story. Then again, perhaps he had just run out of ideas. Certainly I detected, in the final email, the wish for an ending, a sense that the time had come to move on – and I suppose I regretted the loss of this regular diversion. When it did come, that last message was short, and more than a little unsatisfactory. It had a cursory, almost telegrammatic quality – an air, not so much of haste, as of exhausted resignation:

Still here. I don't know why you don't answer. I never wanted—

*Well it's too late now. It's here. She is here, with me, I
think forever. Can you imagine that? Forever? I couldn't
have done, before, but now I can. In fact, now I can't
imagine anything else.*
lol
Martin

And that was where it ended. I waited a few days, to see
if there would be more, then I forgot about it. I got a big,
rather interesting project to work on, and I went on a
special diet. The new drugs were more effective than I
had expected and, all in all, life carried on as usual. I didn't
think about Martin again but, once, or maybe twice at
most, I dreamed about the deer larder and that terrified
girl, lying silent in the darkness, and when I woke, I had
to congratulate my former correspondent on having got
to me, if only for a moment.

That, it would appear, was the end of Martin's story,
but mine remained open – no longer told, yet still
unfinished – until a certain Thursday evening, exactly
three months later. I know this to be the case because
I had just returned from my appointment at the hospital
and, in those days, my appointments were on a three-
monthly schedule. I didn't get back from town till quite
late and I was feeling a little low – winter was drawing
in and my hands were worse than usual – but I set to
work as soon as I'd had a bit to eat and got warmed
up. I had a new project to work on, something a little
out of the ordinary. Something into which I was pretty
sure I could work the odd small miracle and I was
determined to make the most of that.

I stumbled across the story while I was on the trail of
something else. That's how it happens, more often than
not: the stuff that stops you dead in your tracks, the little
snippets of information or narrative that seem suddenly

important – those vivid, beautiful or frightening discoveries that seem life-changing – come when you're surfing the Web, looking for something far more pedestrian, or even banal. As it happens, the trail I had been following, for some time, bore almost no relation to my research topic and, when I came upon that final, decisive story, I read it, at first, with only passing interest. Passing interest, idle curiosity even – and then, after a line or two, a growing sense of horror. It wasn't a long article, just a quirky news item, one of those stranger-than-fiction pieces that you only ever half believe but can't put out of your mind for days afterwards. Usually, such pieces have an obvious whiff of exaggeration or invention about them – it's not that they are out-and-out lies, it's just that they are so loosely based on the known facts that they might as well be fictions. Not this one, though. This one was true, more or less. I knew that even before I knew what I was reading.

As I say, it wasn't a long piece, and it was quite badly put together, wordy and rambling and stylistically weak. Real cub-reporter stuff. In short, it told the story of a man who had been found, naked and alone and quite obviously mad, squatting on a raised beach on the isle of Jura. Someone had seen him from a ferry boat and called the police; subsequently, the man, who could not or would not speak and appeared not to have eaten or slept for some time, was taken to a hospital on the mainland, where he was later identified as Martin Crisp, a university lecturer from Reading, who had been renting a house on the island over the summer. The piece concluded with two quotes, the first, from a local man, who said that Mr Crisp had been touched by the fairies, and it would be a long time before he ever came right, the second, from one of the hospital staff, who said that Mr Crisp was still unable to speak but, though it was obvious that something terrible had happened to this man, there was no clinical reason for his condition. When asked to elaborate further, the doctor – whose name, by what seemed to me a chilling coincidence, was Elizabeth Marsh – remarked that she had never before had a case quite like this one. 'It's not that Mr Crisp *can't* talk,' she said – and I pictured my own Dr Marsh saying this – 'But it seems to me that he's said what he wanted to say and now he's waiting for his answer.'

The Cold Outside

When the cancer came back, I wasn't surprised. I was upset for Caroline, knowing she'd have to be told eventually, and I was bothered about how Sall would take it, after last time. I was even sorry for Malky, because finding reliable drivers was difficult and he'd always been a good boss. Still, I wasn't surprised, not when they told me. I'd been expecting something to go wrong since the summer, when Sall and I had talked about flying over to Montreal to see Caroline and meet her new boyfriend, then given up on the idea. Sall knew I was keen, of course: Caroline had always been Daddy's little girl and, ever since she'd left, it had been an effort to hide how empty the house felt without her – an effort I'd sometimes failed to make. Sall probably knew as well as I did that I was on borrowed time, so to begin with she had gone through all the motions of planning the trip, but then she'd started talking about how expensive it was, and how tiring it would be for me, having to drive over to Glasgow then sit on the plane for seven hours and then, after all that, there was immigration and customs, which took forever. The way she spoke, it was as if she'd done the journey herself, but she hadn't. She'd never even left Scotland, and all that talk was just stuff she'd picked up from Caroline, who'd been back three times in the six years since she'd got the job in Montreal. Not long before her last visit, though, she had met this new boyfriend and had started making a big thing about how it was our turn to go over there.

'I understand it's a long way,' she'd said. 'But you'll love it when you get here. You'll see. It'll be a nice holiday.

Besides Jim keeps asking me if you really exist. He thinks I made you up.' She'd laughed, but the invitation was real, even if she didn't look at Sall when she said it, but kept her eyes fixed on me. She was content to work around her mother for my sake, now that the two of them didn't have to live in the same house. For her, it was all about careful management, about avoiding those occasions when something might be said that couldn't be taken back. Even before she'd left, she had come and gone like a ghost, just so she didn't have to be with Sall. I'd never really understood why. I once overheard Caroline say that her mother could start a fight in an empty room, but that wasn't altogether fair. The two of them just weren't able to sit together without arriving at some kind of disagreement or misunderstanding. It was a mismatch of personalities, something that happened all the time, in all kinds of situations. It was only shocking when it happened between a mother and her child.

Whenever Caroline extended one of those vague invitations, I wanted to tell her that we'd come over as soon as we could, but Sall always got in first. 'We'll see,' was all she'd say, and then she would set to work, undermining the idea. That was what she had done during the summer, making up excuses and problems and eventually talking the trip out of existence, till we ended up driving down to Hertfordshire instead, for a sad fortnight of rain and teashops with Sall's brother Tom and his second wife. I'd understood what was going on and I told myself it was probably for the best, what with the history between them; still, that so-called holiday was more of an upset than I'd expected. At first, I just put it down to the usual disappointment with Sall's games and the way I never seemed to be able to stand up to her, but somewhere in the midst of it all, wandering around a grimy little bric-a-brac shop in Stevenage, I realised that I'd given up the last chance I would ever have to visit Montreal.

So the knowledge was already there, sitting at the back of my mind, waiting to come true, when the doctor told me. I was almost ready for it: almost accepting, the way you're supposed to be in all the stories they tell about dying. Not completely, but close, just waiting to hear how it was going to be, so I could walk out of the surgery and get on with what was left of my life. I had a matter of months, the specialist thought, and the idea crossed my mind that I could do anything I liked. I was free. Except that there wasn't anything I wanted to do that much, other than seeing Caroline, and I knew what Sall would say to that now. I'd heard it all before: how I had never had any time for anybody but my little girl, how I'd spoiled her rotten. To hear Sall talk, you'd have thought that what happened between them was all my fault, but I looked back in my mind's eye and I tried to find a picture, one reliable image of the two of them happy together, and I couldn't. Not even when Caroline was a baby. I could see me standing at the window in the back bedroom, rocking her to sleep and singing her Christmas carols, because they were the only songs I could remember, and I could see the two of us, when Caroline was six, going around and around on the horses at Flamingo Park, while Sall sat off by herself, watching, a curious, slightly bewildered look on her face, as if she was ashamed or embarrassed about something. I could see Caroline laughing at my bad jokes as we drove to school in the morning, and I saw us making a row of snowmen in the garden — four of them, all identical. That was why I liked driving, and that was why I didn't mind going back on the road so soon, because when I was out there, on my own, I would look at those pictures in my head and I would be happy.

Anyhow, the day after I got the diagnosis, I was back at work, hauling treacle. I would have been willing to stay home for another day or two, but when Malky called, that first evening, Sall told him I was fine, and I'd be back in the morning. I didn't blame her for that; we needed the money. I suppose I should have been disappointed that she didn't want me at home, at least for a little while, but I wasn't. I knew it wasn't really her fault. She just didn't know how to deal with that kind of thing. Even before we left the surgery, I could feel her shifting away, the way she always did whenever there was a problem. She slipped away into her own separate place, like she had done when we were first married and things weren't what either of us had expected, or during the long weeks after Caroline left, and we were left stranded, speechless and unable to touch or even look at one another, alone together with the quiet of an empty house and a shelf's worth of pale photographs in the matching set of Shaker-style frames that Sall had bought at the Sue Ryder.

So I'm not blaming her. I was just as glad to go back on the road and not have to sit moping about the house. Besides, I've always liked pulling treacle. Molasses to give it its proper name. Every now and then, I drive around the countryside, delivering the warm, dark slop that farmers use to supplement the fodder for the cattle, mixing the treacle in with barley to make a sweet malty mix that the beasts can't get enough of. I like going out on the farms, all quiet and lonely in the middle of the day; I like talking to the farmers and listening to their stories, men who have never been anywhere in all their born years save these hundred acres of ground, grown men haunted by their own holdings. To be honest, I like hauling treacle more than anything else. There are times when it's so thick and dark and solid you could walk on it, and we have to work hard to get it pumped out and into the big tanks that are usually so old and creaky that you don't think they'll hold. Sometimes they don't. On a really warm day, one of the pipes, or maybe the wall of the tank, will give way, and there will be treacle everywhere: treacle and the smell of treacle that makes you dizzy, it's so sweet and strong.

It was hard work, but it was good being busy. It gave me less time to dwell. And I knew, when I started out that winter's morning, that I'd feel better coming home with a full day's work under my belt, knowing that I wasn't quite used up. I thought about that all day, driving round the farms in the frosty light, about how I would keep going till I couldn't go on any more. All a man has is his work and his sense of himself, all the secret life he holds inside that nobody else can know. That was how it had always been, even at home: my real life was separate from the day-to-day business that Sall knew or cared enough to make decisions about. It wasn't that I didn't love her, at least to begin with; we got on well enough in the first few years. It was just that we'd always been private people, in our different ways. That was probably what made it possible for us to stay together after Caroline moved away. We knew how to keep ourselves to ourselves, a skill we had perfected over years without even knowing how completely we had mastered it.

It was late in the afternoon, the sun just going down over the fields, the last of the light filtering through the trees and shrubs along the road by the old hospital. The first green of evening, my mother had always called it, sitting on the back step at home, watching the Peruvian lilies and the montbretia fade into the gloaming. I was never sure if that was a phrase of her own, or a quote from something, some radio drama, say, or a children's book she'd read to me in the days before memory. Usually, if I got home early, this was my time. While Sall made herself busy in the kitchen, I would sit in the dining room with the paper spread out on the table, or I would listen to the radio, staring out at the garden and fiddling with the dials to get a better signal. That day, though, I had pulled a long run, only just finishing up at Jacob's Well Farm when the dark set in. It had been a good day, but I knew I wasn't supposed to overdo it, so I was happy enough to say my goodbyes to Ben Walsh, who used to run Jacob's Well with his dad, and keeps it going himself now, his wife gone, no kids, both his parents dead. He had been living alone like that for some years by then, which was maybe why he paid so much attention to the few people he encountered. That day, it was attention I could have done without, but then he wasn't to know what my troubles were. He offered me a cup of tea, but didn't seem to mind when I told him I'd better get on back. He gave me a solemn little smile and shook his head. 'How's the missus?' he said. 'Keeping all right?' He always talked about Sall as if she were an invalid – which, in a way, she was.

'Can't complain,' I said.

'That's good.' He gave me an odd, shy look. 'Still, if you don't mind me saying, you're looking a bit under the weather yourself.'

'Oh, no,' I said. 'I'm fine.'

'Yes?'

'I'm a bit tired, I suppose,' I said. 'It'll pass.'

He nodded. He was curious and, I think, genuinely concerned, but he knew not to pursue it. 'Well, I hope so,' he said. 'You take care of yourself. You don't want to be coming down with something, right before Christmas.'

I managed a smile. 'You can say that again,' I said. 'Anyway, this is the last of it, before the holidays. I'll get a good rest then. You take care, too.' I shook his hand and got back into the rig. For a moment, I wished I'd said yes to the tea and stopped, not to talk about anything in particular, but to keep company with the man for a while. I couldn't imagine that his Christmas would be that festive, with just him and the animals.

Then again, I couldn't imagine much of a Christmas for myself, now that everything was decided. I wasn't looking forward to the quiet of the holidays, or having to go through the motions with Sall, which she would want to do, because – well, it was Christmas. Maybe Caroline would ring, sometime in the middle of the afternoon, making the call first thing, so she could get on with the rest of the day knowing she'd done her duty. I hadn't said anything to her about the cancer, of course. I'd considered telling her the first time, but it would only have worried her, and then she might have felt duty-bound to come over. This time, I didn't even give it a second thought, because I knew for sure that I was going to die and I wanted to do it in my own way. I wanted to let go of life with some kind of grace, or at least with some attention to what was happening, instead of just sitting quietly in the middle of some great drama between Sall and Caroline about what they thought I should do. That was how it had been for so much of my life: I hadn't missed any of the big events but, at the same time, I hadn't felt entirely present while they were happening. Those last few weeks, though, I noticed everything. Like the way time would catch up with me all of a sudden, and I'd see myself opening a letter, or making a cup of tea: see myself from above, doing these ordinary little things and taking an odd pleasure in them, though I can't say why, unless it was because it might be the last time I'd open a letter or make a cup of tea.

I'd notice things out on the road, too, things I'd seen a thousand times before and had liked without knowing why. Little details and imaginings I'd dismissed all my life as plain silliness suddenly became important. Like that stretch of road on the way back from the Glasgow run, when I would pass the turn-off for Larbert. I used to see it all the time: a blue road sign and a row of cherry-cola street lamps running off into the distance: Larbert, A9. It was odd, how much I liked that sign. I'd never had reason to go to Larbert. We didn't do any runs in that direction, but then maybe that was why I'd always liked the name. Larbert. It sounded like a place where the teenage years went on forever, all grey days by the water and strange-tasting sweets that fizzed in your mouth, making you think of the possibility of sex. Not that I had ever known much about sex as a teenager, other than what I saw in films and the oddly pleasurable discomfort I felt when Rita Compton visited my sister.

That was the kind of stuff that was running through my head when I came across the boy, a few hundred yards into the woods, in the first of the heavy rain. I was thirty miles from home when it started, a thick sleet that might turn to snow later, or might come to nothing; it was already dark enough for headlights but, as I came into the woods, ducking under the beech trees, it was like entering a little theatre, the lights flickering across the darkness, the woods dark and still like a backdrop. I'd always liked that about the woods, the way they suddenly closed in on me as if a story were about to be told. Like when I was a boy, and the announcer on *Listen with Mother* would say: 'Are you sitting comfortably? Then I'll begin.' Usually the road was empty, with maybe the odd set of headlamps – not a person, not even a car, just an effect of the light – streaming past in the opposite direction. But that night the story contained another character, though he wasn't a character from any of the children's books I knew.

To begin with, I thought he was a woman. Maybe I wouldn't have stopped if I'd known otherwise. He certainly looked like a woman: a black dress, no coat, fishnet stockings, high-heeled ankle boots, shoulder-length wavy hair. She was walking slowly, towards the far end of that little avenue of beech trees and I couldn't make out much, but when my lights picked her out, she turned, and I saw there was something odd about her, something heavy. Not that I guessed right away that she was a boy. It was dark and rainy, and then, when I saw her properly, I was distracted by the bruises on her face: the bruises, the mess her hair was in, the dark stain that might have been blood on her right leg, just below the hem of the dress.

I didn't pick up hitch-hikers much. I had done, in the early days, and I'd enjoyed the chat, most of the time. Not always, but enough to make it worthwhile. More recently, though, I'd preferred being alone in the cab, with my own thoughts for company. Some nights, coming home in the dark, reeling off the narrow roads that ran to Perth or St Andrews, remembering the way by my own land-marks, the hedges and dry-stane dykes and the spaces between them that other people didn't even notice, tight angles of holly or lamplight as I came through a town, I would realise, with a pleasant rush of surprise, that I was fond of myself as I was, fond of my life, and yet, at the same time, not that worried about having to let it go. I had got past the stage when company seemed like a good thing on the road, and I have to admit that I thought about driving on that night, even after I'd noticed the gash on her leg. I didn't need complications, and by then, every-thing that wasn't part of the usual schedule had come to seem unnecessarily complicated. Nevertheless, I made myself stop, and I pulled up alongside her – still thinking of this person on the road as a woman, possibly a woman in real difficulty – just to check, at least, that she was all right. I rolled down the window and leaned across to the passenger side. 'You look like you ran into some trouble,' I called out, trying to make myself heard above the engine and, at the same time, not to be so loud that I might frighten her.

The moment I put on the brake, she stopped walking – and that was when I realised that she wasn't a woman. She looked up, and I could see it in everything about her: the way she stood, the darkness in her face, the heaviness. It was a boy, not a woman. Not a man either, just a boy of eighteen or twenty, fairly thickset and not at all feminine. When he looked up at me, I saw the fear in his face, behind the mass of wet make-up and mascara,

a fear that he wanted, but couldn't quite manage to hide.
'I'm OK,' he said, but he stayed where he was, stock-still,
waiting.

'Where are you headed?' I said, switching off the ignition
and trying to keep the surprise out of my voice.

'Home,' he said; then he mumbled something else that
I couldn't make out.

'What was that?' I said.

He shook his head. He seemed desperate, though I
wasn't sure if he was desperate to be helped or to be left
alone – at least, not until he spoke. 'I'll be fine,' he said.

I knew then that he wanted to trust me enough to get
him home safe and dry. I also knew that he didn't trust
anybody, not right at that moment, anyhow. 'Well,' I said.
'I'm Bill Harley. I'm on my way home from a long run
delivering molasses and it's nearly Christmas, so I'm not
going to leave you out here in the dark.'

Something changed in him then. Maybe it struck him
as funny that I was talking about molasses, but he seemed
to soften. He moved closer to the cab and tried to see
inside. 'I'm going home,' he said. 'It's just down this road.'
He looked up into my face. 'I'll be fine,' he added, though
he sounded less convinced than before.

'Oh, come on,' I said. 'Do yourself a favour. We'll get
you home and you can get cleaned up.' I swung the
passenger-side door open.

The boy nodded. I suppose he'd weighed me up and
decided it was worth the risk. Or maybe he was just past
caring and the promise of shelter was more than he could
resist. 'All right,' he said. 'It's very kind of you.'

I nodded, then waited while he climbed into the
passenger seat. He had a bit of trouble with that, what
with the dress and the high heels that I assumed he wasn't
used to, but finally he got himself settled and pulled the
door shut. I looked at him a moment in the gold light
from the overhead, then I started up the engine as casually

as I could. 'Well,' I said, raising my voice so he could hear me over the noise. 'Where are you headed?'

'Coaltown?'

I nodded and turned back to the road. It was a good twenty miles to Coaltown, not just down the road, but I had to pass it on my way home anyway. 'OK,' I said.

'You know it?'

'I used to work there,' I said. 'Long time ago.'

'Well,' he said. 'You'll not find it much changed. I guarantee you that.'

'I don't suppose I will,' I said, letting off the handbrake. As I did, I caught sight of the gash on his leg. It looked nasty, but the bleeding seemed to have stopped. There was dirt all over his legs and hands, dirt and blood dried into the mesh of his fishnet stockings. His face was badly bruised, as if someone had punched him several times. I turned away and looked back to the road, but I knew he'd noticed me looking at him.

'I'm all right,' he said. 'Just a few cuts and grazes.'

I shook my head. 'It's a bit more than that,' I said.

He let out a short, hard laugh, as if I'd made some joke at his expense. 'I suppose it is,' he said – and I detected something in his voice, more of a drift than a slur, that suggested he might be on something.

'Well,' I said. 'It's none of my business. But I've got a first-aid kit in the box behind you.' I tilted my head towards the back. 'If you want to get yourself sorted out.'

'I'm fine,' he said. 'But thanks, anyway.' He shot me a quick glance, then looked away. 'I've had worse.'

'Really?'

'Rules of the game,' he said. 'It's not as bad as it looks. I just went to the wrong party.' He glanced out at the wing mirror. 'I suppose it was a mistake, going for the Aileen Wuornos look.' I had to think about that for a moment, before I remembered who he was talking about, and he must have seen the realisation dawn in my face, because he laughed again, louder and more confident this time. 'Don't worry, Bill,' he said. 'I didn't bring the gun.' I had to smile at that. 'Well,' I said. 'There's a relief.'

He laughed again, but this time his laughter was good-humoured and warm and I was suddenly glad that I'd stopped. 'So,' he said. 'Where are you headed, Bill Harley?'

'Home,' I said and suddenly I realised that I didn't want to think about home, at least for the moment. I wanted to be out on the road still, out on the road on a winter's night, with no set destination, passing the time with someone I'd never see again.

'Ah yes,' he said. 'Home.' He dwelled on the word for a moment before moving on. 'Soon be Christmas,' he said.

'Not long.' I looked over at him; he was watching me, attentive, taking me in, maybe searching for something that he thought I wanted to keep hidden – and I suddenly had an image of Caroline, of how she had watched me like that sometimes when she was younger, hoping for a clue to what lay behind the facade that she thought I was working so hard to maintain. Maybe that was what made me say what I said next, surprising myself, and the boy. I didn't say it very loudly, and I wasn't really speaking to him, but it was loud enough to be audible over the noise of the engine. 'One last Christmas,' I said. 'Better make the most of it, eh?'

It wasn't what I'd intended to say, though I wasn't sorry I'd said it. Still, I had no wish to pursue the notion any further, now that it was out – and I think he understood that because, after allowing just enough space for what I might say next, he let it go without another word, and we drove on in silence, staring out from our separate places into the sleety darkness, our faces filling with light from time to time as a car passed from the opposite direction. It was slow going, then, but the silence didn't bother me; if anything, it felt strangely comfortable, like having a passenger in the cab and being alone at the same time. After a while, though, the boy picked up the conversation, dropping casually into the kind of slow-moving, pointless talk that goes on between people of goodwill who don't know each other well: stuff about football – I was surprised by that, though I suppose I shouldn't have been – and some documentary he'd seen on television. It could have been anybody in the cab with me, to begin with at least, but then he started talking about other things, minor stuff about his schooldays mostly, only it was funny and good-humoured and all the time I knew he was really talking about something else altogether, some other story about himself that he wanted to tell, not out of need, but because it was interesting. Like his memory of the school atlas that he'd been given in geography class – how he had loved the way the world was all mapped out, all the colours and lines and borders perfect and just, so that it looked like the kind of world it would be a pleasure to inhabit, an utterly fictional world where you could never be lost, because everybody and everything belonged somewhere. I enjoyed that, for as long as it lasted, partly because it felt new, to be driving along like this, talking to a boy in a dress and runny make-up, but mostly because he was such good company. When we finally reached the turn for Coaltown, he leaned forward in his seat slightly. 'If you drop me here, that'll be fine,' he said.

I shook my head. I didn't want to just drop him in the dark, on another stretch of featureless road. 'I'll take you to your door,' I said. 'It's no trouble.'

'Thanks, Bill,' he said. 'But I'd rather walk from here. No offence.' He looked over at me and, even out of the corner of my eye, I could see he was hoping he hadn't somehow insulted me.

'None taken,' I said, but I turned off the main road and carried on a few hundred yards towards the coast before I stopped.

'Thanks,' he said.

'Don't mention it,' I said.

He put his hand on the door, as if to go, then he turned and smiled, not at me so much as at something that had just crossed his mind. 'It's not how you think it is,' he said. I felt uneasy, as if he were breaking some prearranged code and started telling me a secret that I wasn't supposed to know. 'I'm happy with how things are, most of the time,' he said, and it was as if he were talking to someone else, trying to persuade them that what he was saying was true. Someone else, or himself, or a little of both. 'So that question in your mind,' he said. 'You might as well forget it.'

I nodded, but I didn't say anything. I really didn't want to make something of it, even if there was a question in my mind, because it wasn't the question he probably thought I wanted to ask. I didn't need to know about his life, or what he did sexually, or what he wanted to do, or any of those things. I certainly didn't want to know what the wrong party had been, or how he had come about his cuts and bruises. Some part of me was curious about him, but it was his happiness I was curious about – because I thought he wanted me to imagine him as happy, and I wondered why it mattered to him. Or maybe I was just surprised that he seemed to believe that happiness was possible – and probably that was why I asked him the question I thought he wanted to hear because, even on such short acquaintance, I liked him and I wished him safe, at least. It was a piece of shorthand, I suppose, for all the other questions, the ones about happiness and being alone and going home safe. It was also nothing at all. 'Do you know what you're doing?' I said.

The boy laughed. 'Never,' he said, with a little too much emphasis. 'But you have to pretend, Bill.' He regarded me for a moment. 'If you don't pretend,' he said, 'you're lost.'

I had no idea what he was talking about, but I understood anyway. He couldn't do anything else, was what he meant. He couldn't do anything else, and neither could anybody else. 'Well,' I said. 'You be careful now.' It sounded a bit lame, but then he knew what I meant by that, too.

He slid down off the seat and turned back to me. 'You too, Bill,' he said. He'd said my name again, and I suddenly realised that I didn't know his. 'Have a good Christmas,' he said.

'You too,' I said. Then I slipped into gear, let off the handbrake and pulled away, leaving him there in the slow, dark sleet. I didn't look back through the wing mirror so I didn't see what he did next, and it wasn't until I was some miles further down the road that I realised that he hadn't wanted to talk about himself at all, he was just giving me something back, and I felt sorry not to have understood it at the time, but glad too because, out on the road, in the cold, any gift is better than nothing.

After I dropped him the weather cleared a little and the last ten miles took next to no time. I liked that final stretch, the road going straight along the coast for a while, the water big and empty to the south, the fields and low hills above spotted with light here and there from farmsteads and faraway cottages. By the time I turned off and climbed the rise towards home, the sleet had stopped altogether; a few miles further on, I came within sight of my own village, not much more than a row of houses straggling along a back road, a brief distraction on the way to somewhere else. The lights here always seemed dull and brownish in comparison with the fairy-tale silver of the lights I'd seen from the high road and it struck me, sometimes, coming home late, that I knew the place too well. I knew all the stories. I knew what the people were doing behind those windows. I could see the abandoned dinner tables and the stone sculleries, the muddy boots on the doormat, the piles of newly opened letters on the sideboard, the silent men sitting in worn armchairs in the kitchen, watching television.

When I reached my own cottage, I parked the rig in the lay-by opposite and let myself in through the side gate, coming across the garden to the back door, which was always left unlocked. The house was silent, almost dark; the one lamp burning was in the dining room, a room we hardly ever used, preferring to eat in the creaturely warmth of the kitchen. I wasn't surprised that Sall was in there, though: that was where we kept the things that her real life was made from, the best china and the family albums and the framed pictures from what she probably thought were better days. I opened the back door and went through the kitchen as quietly as I could – quieter, those last months, than I'd ever been before, as if the promise of death had revealed a carefulness in me that I'd never suspected – and I found Sall sleeping in the big armchair by the fireplace, a magazine on the floor by her feet, an empty mug cradled in her lap. Asleep like that, unguarded, her head leaning heavily to one side, she looked old and tired, but at least the worry that usually haunted her face was gone and, as I stood watching her, it struck me that she was dreaming. I knew she would be upset if she woke up and found that I'd come home while she was sleeping, but I stood a moment longer, watching her dream and wondering how she had spent the day, what she had thought about, what she had done. After a moment, though, I felt uncomfortable spying on her like that, and I walked back through to the kitchen, to let her rest.

It was colder than ever now, but the sky had cleared and a bright moon had emerged from the clouds, cold and white in a pool of indigo sky right above the garden. I put the kettle on, then I stepped outside and stood on the patio, looking over the fields to the stand of trees and the long stone wall that I knew were just beyond, black and irrefutably solid in the darkness. It was almost completely silent: from time to time, a dog barked at the end of the road, or the odd gust of wind caught in the beech hedge by Sall's flower border; then, after a minute or so, the kettle began to sing quietly and, as I felt the silence slipping away, I tried to capture it all, to drink it all in, before Sall woke up and I wasn't alone any more. This was my life, these were the times when I was true: in these half-hours here and there when I felt alone in the house, or those fleeting moments out on the road, when I opened a gate and crossed an empty farmyard, a stranger, even to myself, in the quiet of the afternoon. The best part of the day was getting up at dawn and going down to the cool, grey kitchen, the dark garden waiting at the door like some curious beast strayed in from the fields, a casual attentiveness in the coming light that seemed ready to include me, as it included everything else, in a soft, foreign stillness. That was the best, because I knew Sall would stay in bed until after I left, whether she was awake or not – though times like tonight were almost as good. It had become more frequent of late, this coming home and knowing Sall was asleep somewhere, the magazine she had been reading slipped to the floor, a mug of tea cooling on a side table. It felt like coming home to another house, a place full of secrets, a childhood still there, intact among the green shadows under the stairs. First love, too – though not for Sall, after all, even though I'd never known anyone else, or not in that way. No: if thirty years of marriage and bringing up a child had taught me anything, it was that through everything, through all the Christmases and birthdays, through all the mishaps and misunderstandings, almost nothing had been shared. Everything that happened had happened to us separately and, afterwards, in my own mind, it all had a strangely abstract feel: a marriage inferred from picture books and Saturday matinees, a love that didn't quite materialise, a series of other lives that had involved me for a while then shied away, the way an animal does when you make the wrong move and remind it of what you really are.

The kettle was whistling now, and I thought to leave it, so that Sall would have to get up and turn off the gas. That way, I could pretend I hadn't seen her sleeping. It felt too close, seeing her like that. It was as if I were breaking the rules we had worked for years to set up, a system of small courtesies and avoidances and slow, fluid conversations that ran for days, pieces of hearsay and local news passed back and forth over meals and cups of tea to cover the bewildered quiet that had fallen upon us. It was awkward sometimes, but it did work and it was better than any of the possible alternatives. For a moment, I thought of the boy on the road and wondered if it would ever come to this for him, if he would ever come home and find someone he cared for, but no longer loved, asleep in an armchair. It was a tender thought, I suppose, but it wasn't sad, or sentimental, and it didn't have anything to do with death. It was just a notion, passing through my mind, while I waited for the kettle to stop whistling.

Only it didn't stop and, after a while, I walked back inside and turned off the gas myself. At exactly the same moment, Sall came through, her eyes bleary, an odd, faraway look on her face. She seemed surprised to see me, as if she hadn't heard the kettle at all but had just woken up in what she thought was an empty house – and it struck me, for the first time, how difficult it would be for her, having me die first.

'You're back,' she said. It sounded like an accusation. She glanced at the clock, but she didn't say anything else.

'It was a long run,' I said. 'I just got in.'

She nodded. 'I haven't made you anything,' she said. 'I didn't know when you'd be finished.'

'It's all right,' I said. 'I'm not that hungry.'

She gave me a quick, scared look. 'You've got to eat,' she said.

'I'll have an omelette or something later,' I said. 'I was just making coffee, if you want some.'

'I'll make it,' she said. 'You sit down. You've had a long day.'

I nodded, but I didn't move. The door was still open, just enough that I could smell the cold outside, and I heard the dog barking – further away now, it seemed, at the darker end of the road that ran past our house and into the hills, past the gold lights of farms and dairies and narrow sheep-runs through the gorse where snow was probably beginning to form, real snow this time, not the cold sleet I'd driven through in the woods where I met the boy. For a split second – no more – I wanted to get back in the rig and drive on, up into the darkness, into the origin of the approaching blizzard, just to be alone out there, the way that boy had been alone in the woods. Then, with Sall watching me curiously, and perhaps fearfully, I let that thought go and went through to the living room, where the curtains were already drawn and the night was nothing more than a story to be told by a warm fire, with the radio humming quietly in the background, so the world felt familiar and more or less happy, like the future that seemed possible when you didn't think about dying, or the pastel-coloured maps in a childhood atlas that you couldn't help but go on trusting, even when you knew that they no longer meant what they said.

A Winter's Tale

Back when I was still spending everything I earned on beer and horses, I'd stop in at Davy Stamper's on Saturday afternoons. Davy had been a friend of my dad's, and we stayed in touch after my folks died: I'd go round most weekends and sit in the back room of the shop, drinking sweet, milky coffee and listening to him talk about the old days. I loved those aimless conversations, though I pretended I was just killing time till they chalked the last results up at the bookie's. I loved the man, too, which surprises me, looking back. Davy was an old man with bad teeth and thick tufts of grey hair in his ears and nose; sitting there in his technician's coat, he looked like a captive bear in a circus show. He was slow and heavy, and his conversation wandered at times, but I loved him anyway, partly because he was the last connection to a world I had lost. He was smart, too, in his way: he wore that grey technician's coat because that was what he was: a technician, an old-style repairman. Once, that was all he'd done, and the shop still showed the signs of its former life, with radios and electrical appliances piled up everywhere, waiting to be resurrected or stripped down for parts. Latterly, though, it looked more like a flea market: there were stacks of bad crockery everywhere, and Formica tables groaning with the kind of bric-a-brac that nobody ever wanted. In winter, the place seemed grey and worn and there was always that burnt lampshade smell that I remembered from the prefabs, a mix of singed dust and grease, and just a hint of slowly cooking Bakelite. Still, Davy didn't seem to mind. When I went round, he would have a radio playing in the back room, and I'd see the warm gold of the dials as I went in, the only real colour in the whole place that hinterland of foreign voices talking about who knew what, in some far-off studio in Helsinki or Rome.

By that last winter, those Saturday afternoons had become a ritual, and we'd sit talking for hours amidst the Hoover bags and spare parts and gutted radios. The day I'm thinking of, though, he'd asked me to mind the place while he went to visit his sister. She'd been ill, and he felt guilty that he hadn't seen her for a long time, so he was going out there on the bus, with a box of chocolates and a scraggy poinsettia, to wish her Happy Christmas. He wasn't looking forward to it, though: Ella was older than him and from what I'd heard she'd always been a bit of a tyrant. Maybe that was why he seemed so nervous when I was seeing him off, a freshly scrubbed ten-year-old with soap behind his ears reawakened in that old man's body. He'd put a tie on, and a clean cardigan; he'd even polished his shoes.

'You look smart,' I said. I'd made an effort to get out of the pub by half-one, so he could get away in plenty of time.

He grimaced, but I think he was pleased with the compliment. 'Got to make an effort,' he said.

I nodded. 'Keeps you young.'

He grunted, but he didn't have time for banter: his bus left at five past two. 'Help yourself to coffee,' he said, as he shambled out; then he looked back and grinned. 'And don't run off with the takings.'

After he left, I went through the back. I planned to take it easy, maybe take a look at the paper, while the world drifted by outside. It had been wet all morning, but people were hurrying up and down the street doing their Christmas shopping, or just hanging around in doorways after the pub, smoking and chatting. A gang of boys came marching down the road, calling out to passers-by; I recognised a couple of them from the Maple Leaf. A girl I had a thing with once, Cathy Taylor, was going by and one of them called something to her, though I didn't hear what he said. Most girls would have clammed up and hurried away, but not Cathy. She stopped and turned around, as the gang carried on walking, then she called out, loud enough so even I could hear. 'You're no enough of a man for that, sonny,' she sang out, and the boys all laughed. Then they were gone, and Cathy disappeared in the opposite direction, a satisfied look on her face.

After that, it was quiet for a while. It started to rain again, then the rain turned to sleet, icing-sugar-white on the pavement outside, the ghost of snow glimmering through for a moment before it melted. Nobody came into the shop, but that was no surprise, because nobody ever did. Not on a Saturday, anyway. Davy had some regular customers from the old days, but his turnover couldn't have been healthy. Sometimes I wondered why he kept the shop open at all, but I knew how he loved the place and I was pretty sure he would die if he had to give it up. He needed something to do, and he was never happier than when he was stripping down an old radio or TV, trying to figure out how he could make it go.

I wasn't any good at that stuff – but I had my paper, and after I'd fiddled with the radio for a bit, I got a decent music station, mostly Christmassy pop from yesteryear, but company at least. It was going to be a slow afternoon. The street was almost empty now: occasionally someone would hurry past, darting from doorway to doorway, trying to stay dry. At one point, I noticed a dark figure looming at the window, and I thought I had a customer; then I saw that it was just Bobby Crawford. Bobby had been a well-known guitarist once upon a time, but he'd lost it all, and now he lived off his little brother, the one everybody called

Andy C. Andy liked to call himself an entrepreneur, though we all knew his business dealings weren't strictly legal. He looked after his brother, though, and everybody admired him for that. I imagine he knew that his money was mostly going on whisky and dope, but for him, family was family.

Not that he'd have been too happy if he could have seen Bobby from where I was sitting. The boy was off his head, that was obvious. At first he seemed to be looking at something in the window, but after studying him for a moment, I wasn't sure he could see that far. In fact, I wasn't sure he could see anything. He was just *resting*, a bemused smile on his face, his body swaying to and fro in the sleety rain. I thought about going out to see how he was, but before I could move, he was off again, one hand trailing along the window as he headed down the street, towards coffee, or bed, or whatever he thought he was doing next. I watched him go, then I went back to my paper.

It was no good, though. I couldn't read, and I couldn't settle. It got to me, seeing Bobby like that, and soon I was up and pacing about the shop, looking for something to keep me occupied, something practical. It was already starting to go grey outside, and the lights were lit in some of the windows opposite. The Christmas lights had come on too, the ones the council put up along the street every year. It wasn't much of a display, just a few straggling wires of fairy lights in the shape of bells or stars, but it was something, and I could see that the other shops all had decorations of some sort: a plastic tree, a string of lights, even a robotic Santa. Only Davy's stood out, and that upset me, all of a sudden. I knew he *had* lights: he had whole boxes of them, mostly in need of repair, and I remembered him jollying the place up on previous Christmases, so it bothered me that he hadn't made the effort this time around. I didn't like the idea that he'd given up on it all, and I didn't want his neighbours to think he was letting the street down and the idea bugged me so much that I went back to the storeroom and started hunting for something to brighten the place up.

The first lights I found were defective. So were the next. I knew all I had to do was fiddle with the bulbs, or maybe change the fuses, but I just kept on searching instead, and soon I found an old tea chest full of decorations and jumbled up strings of coloured lights, some of which worked when I plugged them in. I carried that lot out and proceeded to tape a string of green and red and yellow lights around one window, then I hung up a couple of fold-out paper bells that might have been manufactured in the 50s, before going back to see what else I could find. That must have been when the kid came in, when I was in the back, because I didn't hear the door. I didn't hear anything in fact, till I came back through, cradling a box of tinsel in my arms, and saw him there, standing by the counter with the knife.

Maybe my head was someplace else right at that moment, and maybe I'm even slower on the uptake than I think I am, but to begin with I didn't realise what was going on. The knife was huge, like something a butcher would use and, to begin with, I thought he'd brought it in to sell. I didn't think I was supposed to buy anything, but I set the box down on the counter and took a step towards the till – and that was when I looked him in the face and saw what he was about. I suppose I surprised him; he'd been expecting an old man and instead he'd found me, and it threw him for a moment. He wasn't much to look at, just a boy really, and maybe he wasn't even that dangerous, but he had the knife and, even though he did skip a beat, it didn't take him long to gather his courage and get back into the script that must have been running through his head when he walked in. 'I don't want to hurt you,' he said, his voice dull and sad-sounding. 'Just give me the money, and I'll get out of your road.'

I stared at him. I didn't really know what to do and, to be honest, I almost laughed, because any fool could see that he'd chosen the wrong shop to rob. As far as I knew, there was nothing in the till but the float. Maybe some takings for the morning, but that wouldn't have come to much. Still, I could see that he was serious: serious about getting the money, and serious about the knife – and it occurred to me that, since he hadn't expected to find me there, he'd been serious about using the knife on Davy if he had to – and that made me angry. I was scared, too, of course, but I was more angry than frightened and, in that instant, I decided he wasn't going to get one penny of the old man's money. Looking back, I realise that I probably sensed something in his body language, or maybe caught a trace of doubt in his eyes, because I'm not a brave person. Far from it. Probably I just saw through his desperate front to a scared boy with drink in his face. A boy like me, in other words. I shook my head. 'Forget it,' I said.

It seemed for one moment that I'd made a big mistake, because something hard came into his eyes and he jerked towards me. I tottered back, just out of range, but there was nowhere for me to go and, if he'd followed through, I'd have been done for. Only he didn't follow through; he hesitated – and that was what saved me, that moment's hesitation.

I'll never know what would have happened if the door hadn't opened at that same moment, but it did, and that was enough to distract him. Even then, he could have finished things, it would have taken so little and I'd seen it done often enough: a glass, a blade, a bottle. It was no big deal; worse things happen in the heat of the moment. So I suppose he just didn't have the heart for it. I suppose, in that instant, he'd weighed up the pros and cons and realised it wasn't worth it – and maybe he was even relieved to have an excuse to get away. Which was what he did, turning tail and barging my one real customer of the afternoon into an old pine table by the door as he vanished into a blur of rain and fairy lights. I didn't know it was over until he was already gone, but I was shaking like a leaf by the time my customer struggled slowly to his feet and turned to me with a big smile on his face. It was Bobby Crawford. I took a step towards him, then I stopped. 'Are you OK?' I said.

He stood a moment, swaying back and forth, smiling; then he nodded. 'I'm fine,' he said. 'I just slipped.' I could hardly understand him; he was slurring his speech so much. 'It's coming on for snow,' he added, by way of explanation. He'd either forgotten the boy with the knife, or he hadn't even noticed him. 'I must have slipped,' he said again, and his smile broadened, as if every fall was a blessing in disguise.

I nodded. I was still trembling, but I didn't want him to see. There was that holy aura around him, that aura of the sainted drunk. 'Maybe we'll get a white Christmas after all,' I said, fighting off the impulse to step forward and take hold of his arm, to stop him swaying. He was doing everything he could to stay upright and any help from me would have shamed him into recognising how far gone he was, and that would have brought him to his knees. 'What can I do you for, Bobby?' I said.

He grinned and shook his head; I think he'd forgotten where he was. Then he straightened up a bit and gave me a serious, man-to-man look. 'I was walking past,' he said. 'And I saw something in the window.' He considered for a moment. 'Thought I'd treat myself. For Christmas. I've been meaning to get one.'

'Right,' I said. 'What was it you saw?'

He stared at me as if he thought this might be a trick question, then he relented. 'Radio,' he said, gesturing vaguely towards the door.

I nodded. 'No problem,' I said. 'I'll just get it out for you.'

He nodded back. He was happy again, the way a child is happy again after a passing scare. 'All right,' he said. 'Thank you very much.' He took a step closer and studied my face. He was looking for someone, or something, and for a moment he thought it was me. Then he saw that it wasn't, and he slid back into his drunkard's courtesy. He looked about him, at the lights and the decorations. 'I really like what you've done with the place,' he said. His eyes had been blue, once upon a time, but now they were faded, like old denim. 'It's very Christmassy.'

After Bobby left, clutching his new radio – a little blue transistor like the one my mum used to have in the kitchen – I went into the back room and put the kettle on. I'd stopped shaking, but I needed something to get me back on an even keel. I fixed some coffee and sat for a while, cradling the cup in my hands, but it wasn't long before I was up and about again, looking out more decorations. It seemed urgent, now, to get the job done before Davy returned. I wanted to surprise him, to give him back the Christmas he'd decided not to bother with this year. Soon I had draped fairy lights across all the tables and hung a whole series of faded paper chains along the shelves. It didn't take that long, and it probably needed more, but I'd run out of stuff to use and, besides, I liked it as it was. Nothing grand, no great show, but it looked fine, as the street darkened, just as the lights across the road and the council's decrepit bells and stars looked fine, local and warm and brave in the gathering cold. In the daylight, none of it would have impressed anybody, but now, as evening closed in, it all came together – here, in Davy's shop, across the road in the baker's window and out along the side streets to the centre of town and the wide land beyond – all these lights came together for a moment in a single fabric of red and green and gold, and it felt like something to be a part of it, if only while darkness fell and the people came in long slow waves, from shops and offices and pubs, making their way home towards the end of a long year and thinking how this Christmas would be perfect for once, perfect and white and clear, like the Christmases they remembered from long ago.

LOST SOMEONE

It's Soul Classics night at the Raven, and I'm at the bar, watching Caroline McElwee and her friend Emma out on the dance floor. Every now and then, she sneaks a glance over at me, and I smile, but she knows I'll not be dancing yet. Not till the DJ plays a slow number, which I've already requested, only I said not to play it till later, when I give him the signal. Caroline is wearing this cream-coloured dress, all full of holes like crochet, and she's looking pretty intense, to tell the truth, but I've got to wait awhile, see what's going to happen with this situation that's just come up. It's most likely nothing, but you never know. Some people walk into a place like this and they're just in for a drink and a dance; some, you don't know why they're here at all, but you know it's not good.

I don't usually do romance. That kind of stuff is fine in a Four Tops song, but it's dangerous when you're trying to deal with all the crap round here. It's − *distracting*. I mean, I *love* those old songs − James Brown, Bessie Banks, Otis − but I also know that beggin' for one more day or asking why somebody don't love you no more is a luxury I can't afford. I've got my hands otherwise full, any day of the week, which today means I'm standing here watching Caroline dance, but I'm also keeping an eye on the two boys who came in about half an hour ago and took up position at the far end of the bar, close to the door. I'm not making a thing of it, but I know who they are, and I know why they're here. The bigger one, Sammy Crane, looks a bit cumbersome and maybe slow on his feet, but that's deceptive. I know, because I've seen him in action. The other one I don't know personally. He's shorter, slighter, but he has that calm in his face, that flat, untroubled look that, if you know how to read it, is like a warning. It's the look you see in a lot of the boys who hang around with the guy I might have a problem with at the moment, a tall skinny speed-freak from the Exeter estate called T. That's his name: T. The name he chooses to go by and if you're ever stupid enough to bring up the name his dear old mother gave him, you maybe won't live to regret it.

As I say, I might have a problem with T, but I don't know for sure. The reasons are complicated, because we go way back but – just *because* we go way back – he's giving me a chance to sort it out myself. Or at least, I *thought* he was. I *thought* he was allowing me a couple of days to take care of said problem, and after that we'd be square. Trouble is, I had a go at sorting it out yesterday and things didn't go according to plan. Which was annoying, sure enough, but I thought I could deal with it later. To be honest, I had a date, so I put it off – and that was probably a mistake. I didn't take the situation seriously enough because I wanted to see Caroline and, anyway, it was just Fat Stan, right? I thought, I'll go see Caroline, and then I'll get round to sorting Stan out later. Cause he's not going anywhere, is he? I mean, where is *Fat Stan* going to go? Hawaii?

Fat Stan. I knew him in school, and I kind of took him under my wing. Protected him from the shit he kept getting into. I even got a bit sentimental about him, like he was the brother I never had, so I've always allowed him too much rope and this time around he's about to hang me with it because, this time around, it involves T, who's *also* like a brother to me – which is to say, he's like the brother I'm *glad* I never had – and so, because it involves T, I have to make sure that this problem doesn't drag on. It's no big deal, I mean, it's not a big money thing, but then, that's not the point. Nobody round here can forget the time T walked into the Crow's Nest and stabbed Pat McDonald while he was playing table football – stabbed him twice, in both kidneys – because he owed T a measly twenty quid. Nobody can forget *that* – and if I'd been thinking straight, I'd have this thing sorted by now. Which I almost did yesterday afternoon, but the fat bastard got away and I didn't follow up, like I should have. I went out on a date. With Caroline. She's the kind of girl thinks you're seeing somebody else if you don't see her every night, and I usually steer well clear of that, only—

I don't know, really. All I can say is, it's different this time. There's just something about her. I mean, I'm not looking for it to last forever, but . . . I see her out on the dance floor and I can't understand why I'm so *happy*. I mean, more than anybody, I ought to know that happy is dangerous. Happy costs you. When you're happy, you look away for a second and – BANG – some bastard like T or one of his trolls waltzes in. It's like earlier, when I was walking over here, I noticed how the leaves looked against the wet black branches on that big tree by the car park, all coppery and golden in the late afternoon sun, like something out of a picture book, and I almost stopped to take a longer look, because it was so pretty. And I felt happy, then, too, which I knew was stupid. I mean, Fat Stan was there, at the back of my mind, and I knew I'd have to find him, quick, but I suddenly didn't care about that and I didn't even think about him again, or not till half an hour ago, when Sammy Crane and his mate turned up.

Now I'm trying not to be too obvious about watching them, when Sammy turns and sees someone coming through the door and it's like he's seen a ghost. And though I don't mean to, that look makes me curious and my eyes follow his, and who do I see but Stan coming across the floor, looking around like he's supposed to be meeting somebody. Next thing, Sammy turns back to me, and I want to explain somehow that I'm not the one Stan is looking for – only I'm wrong, and I don't understand it, because as soon as Stan sees me he heads over in my direction like he's expected or something. He doesn't look scared, it's like he's just coming over to say hello, or maybe do some business, like it's the most natural thing in the world and I'm completely flummoxed. And at that exact same moment, the DJ starts announcing the song I asked for, which is annoying because I'm not ready yet – *Now, here's a special request for Caroline*, he's saying and I glance over and see her turning towards me, smiling, happy – only I can't hold that look, because something is wrong and I need to understand what Stan is doing, walking in here calm as you please, like he doesn't even care about the shit he's got us both into. I need to *understand*, and I can see that Sammy and his mate feel the same way, but I'm distracted by that vision of Caroline turning and the DJ saying, *This is James Brown, from 1961, with 'Lost Someone'*, and then, just as I realise how slow I'm being, Fat Stan takes three or four quick steps towards me, his hand coming up like he's asking a question in school, and something in his hand that I didn't see before flashes silver in the light off the dance floor as it comes down on my neck and James Brown starts to sing, through the sound of someone screaming my name and I think, *this isn't real* – and then I think, *I know that voice*, I know that voice, not from here, but from somewhere else – and I'm trying to answer it, trying to let her know it's all right, everything is going to be fine because *this isn't real*, but I can't find the words and all I can say is a name, though I'm not even sure whose name it is and that's when I know it's too late, when I say the name and then I say it again, and I still don't know who I'm talking to, or if it's even me who's talking, or somebody else, somebody I left behind when the music stopped, and the night wind brushed my face, cool and empty and welcoming, like forever.

Roccolo

Eloise Sereni liked to drink in the afternoon. She would begin at lunchtime, opening the first bottle in the shadowy dining room to the rear of her ground-floor apartment, and drinking steadily while she worked her way through a bowl of salad or pasta. Later, she would open another – something a little lighter and more summery – in place of dessert. She didn't much like sweet things, but she would carry the bottle and a bowl of grapes to the patio, settling into the one corner of shade to pass the hiatus of mid-afternoon staring out at the haze over the sea and listening, through the occasional wave of traffic, for the sound of the water rolling back and forth on the soft grey sand. She would linger a long time over this second bottle, drinking slowly, feeling for the effect. Sometimes, she thought herself happy, very alert and strong with memories of the time when Daddy was still himself, and she was still the prettiest girl in town. Occasionally, she fell asleep in her chair, only to wake an hour later, fuzzy and unsure of where she was, her head full of pure, cruel dreams of the roccolo. On days when she had new tenants, however, she didn't drink at all, but sat in her tiny court-yard at the back of the apartment block, waiting to see who would come. Years ago, all three floors of the apartment building had been inhabited by various members of her family, people she had never known or, if she had, could barely remember. Now, however, the entire building belonged to Daddy. He had acquired it over the years, step by step, and he rented out the upper apartments from April to September, mostly to holidaymakers from England.

Today, a new family was arriving and, though neither she nor Daddy had anything to do with this side of the business – it was all managed by the agency now – she stayed sober through the long afternoon, at least until Beppe's van brought the new arrivals in from the station at Salerno. There was really no reason to interrupt her normal routine, but every time a fresh set of tourists checked in, she sat waiting on her little patio, screened off from the main courtyard behind a stand of oleanders, in the hope that, this time, there would be a boy she could play with. A nice boy of around twelve or thirteen, shy, but not too shy, a boy with blue eyes and dirty blond hair, maybe, who didn't really want to spend two weeks on the Amalfi Coast with his parents, when all his friends were at home.

Now, it was two o'clock, and the town had fallen quiet under the high sun. The old man, Guido, was in his usual place between the street and the courtyard, perched on the edge of a battered chair and craning forward to see who was passing by on the seafront, or which of the Marinelli sisters was working in their father's café across the way. Occasionally, the visitors mistook Guido for a beggar and they would drop a few coins into the chipped enamel cup at his feet, but he wasn't a beggar and, once upon a time, he'd been somebody special, a first-rate hunter and a wise, sinewy man from the stony hillside above the village, skilled with inanimate things and charmed with a rare knowledge of animals and birds. He was the one who had first taken her to the roccolo, way up on the hillside track behind the town, and he had shown her how to hold the bird steady while you pricked out its eyes, quickly and without hesitation, but with great care and accuracy, piercing the bright small button of the eyeball with a silver needle, just so. In those days, Guido had been quiet and elusive; he had shown no interest in what others did, but kept himself to himself, and Eloise had felt honoured that he chose her to share his most secret pleasures. Nobody

used the roccolo any more, of course. Nobody charmed
the birds down from the sky like that, tethering one blind,
plaintive-sounding decoy in the middle of the cold stone
room to lure the others into the nets. Guido had been
the last of his kind and Eloise had never quite understood
why he had chosen her to carry on this ancient tradition.
She couldn't even remember, now, how long it had been
since they started going for their long walks in the hills,
but it hadn't been that long before Guido had his 'accident'. That was how people spoke of it now – *an accident*
– but it was a lie, and they all knew it: one night in the
early spring, as he made his way down from the hills,
Guido had been attacked by several men, and they had
beaten him till his mind was damaged forever. Now, he
sat at Daddy's gate, watching the world go by from somewhere far inside himself, and Daddy let Eloise take him
some food and wine from time to time, so he wouldn't
feel abandoned. He never spoke to her, though. Once, he
had told her all the secrets of the world, all about the
animals in the hills and the ways of the old folk who had
died before she was even born. These days, though, he
didn't say a word, he just gave her a curious look when
she set the tray at his feet, as if he was trying to work out
who she was and why she was being kind to him. He
didn't try very hard, though, and after a moment he turned
away and looked back across the street, to where Angela
Marinelli was clearing tables, in the blue shade of her
father's garden café.

Maybe she had drifted off, or maybe they had just been
very quiet driving in, but Eloise didn't see the new people
until they were unloading their luggage from Beppe's van
in the courtyard. It wasn't a family, just a father and son
and, at first sight, they didn't look very promising, the man
getting under the taxi driver's feet as he insisted on trying
to help, the boy standing off to one side, looking slightly

embarrassed by his father's well-meaning clumsiness –
though Eloise saw, immediately, that this embarrassment
was nothing new, that it was, in fact, a sensation to which
he was very well accustomed. For him, no doubt, incidents
like this happened all the time, and Eloise knew she could
use that later to her advantage. He wasn't a good-looking
boy – in fact, there was something odd about him, an
awkwardness of fit that had contrived to set a teenager's
face on a ten-year-old's body – but she knew right away
that he would be the one. A fortnight earlier, she had
celebrated her thirty-fourth birthday in the usual way, with
two bottles of wine and several glasses of grappa, followed
by a day and a night in bed, but it had never seemed that
there was any real gap in age between her and the boys
she chose each summer, almost always at first sight like this,
and it was no different this time. Like all the others,
this boy had some special quality that only she could
recognise, and the fact that she was almost three times his
age didn't mean a thing, because in her heart, she was still
the impudent, quick-witted girl that Daddy had loved so
much. Besides, she was so good at the game she was about
to play that no difference in age or interest could prevent
it from unfolding exactly as she wished.

She had been playing this game for ten years now,
choosing a boy from one of these English families who
rented Daddy's apartments as a base from which to explore
the coast, taking the local buses to Amalfi or up the steep
winding road to Ravello in the heat of midsummer.
Sometimes she had to wait a long time, but every year
she chose one boy, more or less like this one, to be her
special friend. Sometimes, he would be shy and withdrawn,
the only son in a family of girls, or he would be silly and
happy-go-lucky, but it didn't really matter because it always
ended the same way and, when she first saw him, she
always knew that *this* boy was right for the particular story
she needed to tell. She had to keep it a secret from Daddy,

of course, because he didn't understand, but that wasn't difficult. Daddy kept himself to himself these days, hardly ever coming out of the smaller apartment he occupied at the back of the building, and she barely saw him from one week to the next. Some Sundays, he would shave and put on his old pinstriped suit, then he would come to her door to say it was time for Mass, and she would occasion-ally walk with him as far as the church, leaving him at the door, while she continued along the narrow track, past the little cemetery, to the fields beyond. Of course, she couldn't go with him into the church: that would have been too much. To sit and listen to the priest while the old wives scrutinised her, storing up comments and obser-vations for afterwards, when they walked away together in the growing heat – that was more than she could take. They would talk about Daddy too, of course, and that was worse, somehow, even though Eloise knew that he didn't care. He didn't care, but *she* did, because he was better than any of them, better than all of them put together, no matter what they said.

He didn't understand about the boys, though. He couldn't understand that it was just a story. He thought his beautiful daughter was being cruel for no reason, leading the boys on and teasing them so; he'd never understood that she couldn't help it. She couldn't help it, because that was how the story worked and, besides, she *loved* those boys, each and every one of them. Of course, she knew how important it was to hide that love: at the beginning, so they would fall into her trap and, at the end, because she had to release them back to their families and the world of computer games and maths homework that was all they had ever really known. For a while, she tried to show them a different world, and sometimes it seemed that one or another of them came close to understanding, but they always hurried away eagerly when the time came, back to their mothers and big sisters and safety. That was

a disappointment, of course, but it couldn't be avoided
– and she loved them all just the same, remembering each
of them in turn with a special, private fondness, just as
they would learn to remember, somewhere at the back of
their minds, that strange twelfth or thirteenth summer
when she allowed them the merest glimpse of a beauty
that they wouldn't understand until much, much later,
when they were far away and grown.

She didn't have long to wait before the new boy reappeared in the courtyard. That wasn't surprising, though:
the parents always sent their children out to play while
they unpacked and figured out how the cooker and the
TV worked, and because they had been told not to go
too far, the children would run down into the courtyard
and stand as close as they dared to the gate, wary of Guido,
who would still be there in his battered chair before he
took himself off home, but also eager to see what the
outside world had to offer. So less than half an hour had
passed when the boy emerged and stood a moment at the
top of the stairs, looking out towards the sea. He was
dressed in a dark blue Oxford shirt – a mistake in this
heat – over green and black camouflage trousers. He didn't
notice Eloise to begin with, but he was already aware of
Guido, and he hesitated a moment before descending the
staircase. As he did, Eloise saw the reason for the high-
collared shirt. Some kids would have brazened it out, some
kids wouldn't even have cared, but this boy was sensitive
and, though the blotchy dark-red mark on his neck was
clearly a birthmark, he had never quite been able to forget
it, and it made him awkward and self-conscious, a boy
who wanted to slip away and be off somewhere on his
own, where nobody would see him. At this distance,
however, Eloise couldn't see how large it was, and she
stepped out from behind the oleanders to intercept him
as he came down the steps in a series of hesitant dancing

movements, half-steps, half-hops, obviously putting on a show of nonchalance for Guido's sake, just in case the old man wasn't as self-absorbed as he seemed. 'So,' she said. 'You just arrived.'

The boy was startled – he obviously hadn't seen her – but he recovered quickly and, after a moment, he nodded. 'Yes,' he said. 'My dad brought me.'

As always, Eloise barely allowed him to finish what he was saying. 'And how long will you be here?' she asked quickly, as if this information was important in some way to her own plans.

'Just a fortnight,' the boy replied, looking away. Eloise could see that he was trying to be polite but, really, he wanted to be out on the beach, playing football with the local boys or sitting on one of the big rocks by the jetty, eating an ice cream.

'And was that your father earlier? Helping Beppe with the luggage?'

The boy looked back to her briefly and nodded again.

Eloise smiled. 'Ah,' she said. 'Well, that's a pity. I suppose he must be a great embarrassment to you.'

Now, at last, she had his whole attention. The boy seemed confused, thinking he hadn't understood, or maybe wondering if Eloise had made a mistake – and how was he to know that her English was perfect? Then, after a moment, he shook his head. 'Not at all,' he said. 'Why would you say that?'

Now it was Eloise's turn not to respond. Instead, she stepped closer, to get a better look at the mark on his neck, just visible above the shirt collar. It was a dark-red, mottled stain and what she was seeing, she knew, was only a small part of something larger, something the boy had taken considerable pains to conceal under the dark-blue cotton shirt that he no doubt kept buttoned up, almost to the throat, in all weathers. It was rather beautiful, she thought, this flaw – but Eloise knew she had to save it for a moment, so as not to come in too hard after the remark about the father. She allowed herself a sweet, forgiving smile. If there was one thing she had learned from this game, it was the power of forgiveness. No matter who offended whom, the first to offer forgiveness always won a very special form of advantage. 'So,' she said. 'What's your name, anyway?'

The boy seemed unsure of himself, of course he did, but he decided, finally, that there had been a misunderstanding and, besides, he was *English*, and it would have been rude not to answer. He looked at Eloise for a moment, then he turned away, fixing his eyes on the end of the jetty where the little ferry came in. 'It's Toby,' he said. 'Toby Warren.'

Eloise allowed herself a moment's pause. She could hardly believe it. Not John, not Peter, not Mark or James or Matthew, but *Toby*. It could hardly have been better – and, as the boy turned back to her with a show of what looked like the beginnings of defiance, she allowed herself a faint, almost imperceptible smirk. 'Really?' she said.

'Yes.'

'Toby?' The boy didn't say anything, but Eloise knew she *had* him. 'That's short for Tobias or something, yes?' The boy shook his head slightly and Eloise could see that he was trying to work out if she was just teasing him. 'Well,' she said. 'That's most unfortunate.' She measured out a long enough pause to let her pity sink in. 'What *was* your mother thinking,' she said. 'A good-looking boy like you.' Eloise couldn't help noticing how the boy reddened slightly when she spoke about his mother, and she allowed herself another lingering pause. This was too good to be true. A boy called Toby, with a birthmark, whose parents had recently divorced. She smiled. 'Perhaps she mistook you for a jug,' she said.

Toby looked away again, and Eloise counted another beat before she spoke again. 'Where *is* your mother anyway?'

she said, all innocence − and then, before he could even think of a reply, she reached out and took hold of his shirt collar, pulling it back just enough to reveal the full extent of the dark, raspberry-coloured birthmark. 'What happened to your neck?' she said, keeping hold of the shirt for just a moment longer, then releasing it gently and looking up into his eyes.

The boy stepped back, raising a hand to his throat, as he half turned away. 'It's nothing,' he said. 'It's just a birthmark.' He looked back at her bravely. 'It doesn't hurt, or anything,' he said.

Eloise smiled. 'Well, that's good,' she said. 'But I have to tell you' − and now her face darkened just enough − 'the *girls* won't like it.' It was all in the timing, of course. She had learned that from years of practice. The smile, the expression of sympathy, followed by the throwaway remark, nothing serious, or not really, just enough to sting. An emotional paper cut, so to speak − and then, the salve. She smiled again. 'Well, some girls, anyhow. But then, what do girls like *that* know?'

She looked into his eyes − a kindly, reassuring look − and waited for him to say something, though of course, she knew he wouldn't. He didn't have anything to say, he was just waiting, now, to be released, so he could run to his room and think about what kind of girls *those* girls were. The stupid ones? The pretty ones? Eloise knew which room he would have chosen, of course, and she could picture him now, lying on the bed with the red and green quilt, or sitting in the chair by the side window, blinking back tears. They all did − or at least, the ones she chose did. Maybe that was why she chose them, because they were tender-hearted, and she liked that in a boy. The tough ones weren't so strong, really; they just lacked imagination. 'It was nice to meet you, Toby,' she said. 'I hope we'll see more of each other, while you're here.'

The boy shook his head slightly, then he nodded. 'Yes,'

he said; then he thought for a moment, before adding, in a voice that was almost comically deep, 'I have to go now.'

Eloise smiled. 'Of course you do,' she said, and she didn't speak again till the boy was halfway up the stairs. 'Oh,' she said. 'I should have introduced myself.'

The boy paused, a few steps above where she was standing, and she was happy to see that he took a moment to look back at her. Sometimes they didn't, of course, and that always put a doubt in her mind, but Toby did, and he even gave her a shy, uncertain glance, as if there was something he regretted having said or done. Eloise nodded, allowing him the faintest taste of her approval. 'I am the owner of this building, Toby, and my name is Miss Sereni,' she said. 'But *you* can call me Eloise.'

Eloise spent the rest of the afternoon sitting quietly, enjoying the memory of her small provocation. The look on the boy's face when she talked about girls. The fine tear in his voice when he spoke. She enjoyed the moment as she waited till he reappeared – which was, of course, inevitable because, on their first night, the visitors had to go out and walk about town, reading the menus posted at the doors of every restaurant and deciding, according to taste or budget, where they would enjoy their first meal of the vacation. As it happened, she didn't have long to wait before they emerged from the first-floor apartment, the boy in brand-new jeans and a red sweater now, the father still dressed in the clothes he had worn for the journey. Eloise wondered where the wife was, and who had abandoned whom. The fact that the man hadn't even bothered to change suggested he was enjoying some new freedom – later, he would go back to making an effort, no doubt, either for the boy's sake or his own – and she felt sure she had guessed right in thinking he was a recent divorcee. Though there was always a chance that he was a widower, of course – and that would have been a real gift. Divorce was good, but a dead mother was even better, for obvious reasons, and recently dead was best of all. A recent death is like a door into the heart: with one push, you were *in*, and anything was possible.

She didn't want to be too obvious, of course. All that was required, on this first evening, was the smallest of gestures: a kind word, a smile, an offer of advice on where to find the best pizza. Naturally, they would be going for pizza. They always began with what the children knew best, these summer visitors. Pizza, lasagne, spaghetti alla carbonara. Lukewarm scraps of ravioli in a creamy, yet strangely insipid sauce. It had been a long journey and all they wanted was something familiar. They wouldn't try the strange dishes with *polpi* or artichokes until later, when they had settled in and felt adventurous.

The boy saw her right away. He'd been looking out for her, of course, from the moment his father opened the door and they had stepped out on to the landing at the top of the stairs that led down to the main courtyard. The man was away in his own private zone, however, muttering unhappily into his mobile phone as he descended the stairs, too distracted to be drawn into conversation. He didn't even see Eloise to begin with, as she emerged from behind the oleander and, when he did, he gave no more than a token nod and went on with his conversation. 'Well, that's fine,' he was saying, 'but you have to remember . . .' He broke off to listen to whoever was on the other end of the line, and Eloise didn't hear any more. Meanwhile, she caught the boy's eye and, though it was obvious that he wanted to look away, he couldn't quite manage it. That was when she put on her best smile: a sweet, innocent and, at the same time, almost flirtatious smile that, naturally, took the boy by surprise – though it was nowhere near as surprising to him as the response that, for one moment, he couldn't quite manage to suppress before he and the man passed through the gate and disappeared into the crowded street. He didn't mean to, of course, but he hadn't been able to stop himself, not from waving exactly, but from lifting his hand just a little, as if to wave, or maybe even to touch her arm in passing, as if, in spite of himself, he had suddenly decided that he wanted her to come along.

It was late. Eloise poured herself some wine and sat down at the window of the big sitting room overlooking the street. She felt sorry for the boys, that first day: they were expecting a holiday at the beach, but this wasn't the right place for that; the sand was dusty and grey, not white like the beaches further along the coast, and most mornings the shore would be littered with scraps of paper and foil and old tin-lids smeared with wax from burnt-out candles. Now and again, someone would find a used syringe in the sand, and there would be a minor fuss about how standards were falling, but the truth was, this had never been a suitable holiday destination for the kind of people who rented Daddy's apartments. There were no attractions for the children, just a provincial museum with some old amphorae and scraps of mosaic; there was no marina packed with pleasure craft to take the holidaymakers out to Capri, like they had further down the coast, just the jetty where the ferry to Salerno would put in on its way eastwards. The best you could say about the place was that it made a good base for sightseeing, but that was no use to a boy like Toby, who needed to run outside and find himself immediately on a clean, wide beach with miles of golden sand in all directions.

As luck would have it, however, there *was* the story. When Eloise selected her one boy each year – to have chosen more would have cheapened the romance of it – she allowed them to become part of the story. Sometimes they resisted her, but mostly they fell in quite easily with her plans and there were even times when it all came together, or at least when it came close. People are more impressionable when they are far from home and, besides, what she had to offer was exciting, not just because it went against all the different stories that parents tell about the world, but also because, after the first encounter – after the first insult or snub or sly insinuation of worthlessness – a boy would feel that he had lost face, somehow, and would become secretly desperate to win her over. Sometimes, it was even *too* easy: after all, it is a universal truth that young people get bored on holiday and, when people are bored, they are easy to seduce. Especially if you offer them a secret. Later, they may look back and remember the *gelati* and the picnics, the afternoons on the beach and the evenings in pizza restaurants, but at the time, there's something a little contrived about the happy moments, and in between there were the hours of boredom and frustration, hours of waiting for the grown-ups to be ready, hours of trudging around museums and ancient ruins that somebody had decided were educational. What Eloise offered was a break from all that, the temptation to be wicked and unchildlike. A glass of wine. The faintest hint of a flirtation. A different kind of game than these boys were used to playing – and a different kind of approval. So there were times when it really was too easy, but it was all she had and, besides, she did what she did out of love. Daddy would never understand that, but it was true, nonetheless. Each year she chose a boy she couldn't help choosing: it was decided the moment she saw him hurrying up the steps to the first-floor apartment, excited to be in a new place, or dawdling by the gate, gazing out across the road to the beach, impatient for his parents to finish unpacking so they could get out and about. Naturally, she couldn't let on how she felt; she had to keep up the act and so go through the story step by step, in the appointed order. It could seem a little harsh, perhaps, this first meeting, but now it was over, she had the best part to look forward to. Besides, it had to be done. Eloise knew that Toby would be thinking about her now, as he sat with his father in the pizzeria, and he would think of her later, when he was reading or playing computer games in bed. She had made her presence felt and, over the next several days, she would seep into his life, coming to mind where he least expected her, during a walk on the beach, say, or when he lay down at night, his head full of noises, wanting, but not quite able, to sleep. By itself, the cruelty of this afternoon was nothing, but when they had met in the courtyard, and she had given him that sweet, girlish smile, his whole world had changed. And it was always a surprise, that transformation: the way, when you created an ambiguity, they were always so hungry to be liked, so desperate to see that smile again and so very anxious not to suffer some further humiliation. It constantly amazed her, this need to be loved. If they'd had any sense, they would have walked away on the first day, but they never did. They always came back. They always wanted to be part of the story, no matter what – and that was why she loved them more than anyone else, even more than Daddy.

The next day, Eloise kept to her own apartment, so Toby could settle in. It didn't do to rush things, she knew that from experience. She had to let the boy get his bearings and then, when he had seen how little the town had to offer, the story could begin. Sometimes it could be difficult to draw him in – the family would have plans of their own and some of the parents were surprisingly attentive, but she knew it wouldn't be like that on this occasion. Toby's father had arrived with a briefcase full of papers and, though he probably had every intention of taking his son out for walks on the promenade, or long chatty meals at one or other of the pizza houses along the front, it wouldn't be long before Toby turned up in the courtyard, looking lonely and at a loose end. Sometimes it took a while but, usually, there was a chance to move in and get to know her new friend by the third day of the holiday. On the second day, however, Eloise always stayed out of the way, sitting like a widow in the dark back room of her apartment with a bottle of wine and her old albums for company. She would linger a long time over each photograph, reminding herself of when it had been taken, of how old she was in each of the frames and how old Daddy must have been and, as she turned the pages, she drank steadily till, sometime in the evening, she awoke to the sounds of the passeggiata. After that, she wouldn't be able to sleep for hours, so she would listen to the radio, or read till one or two in the morning. When she did go to bed, she would dream terrible, familiar dreams about Daddy and the day Guido came home from the hospital, his eyes changed, his old strength gone to nothing.

After the restless night, Eloise was usually rather tired on the morning of the third day, and her body would be aching from too much wine; nevertheless, she would carry a straight-backed wooden chair down to the courtyard and she would set it near the foot of the stairs, just a few yards from Guido, who would be stationed by the gate, as always, staring out into the street like some medieval saint waiting for the second coming of Christ. He knew Eloise was there, of course, but, except for that fleeting, puzzled glance when she brought him his food, he never so much as looked at her – and that was the sad part of the story, because they really had been such friends. Eloise remembered how happy it had made her, as a child, to stand with Guido in the roccolo, how she had loved the moment when they came back and found the little stone room full of birds, gathered in a single dark mass in the ancient nets – not a mass of random, lost creatures, but one great body, disconsolate and strangely beautiful, grieving for the sky. The first time, it had surprised her, that moment. She had expected to find it sad, or maybe a little frightening, but it had been so beautiful that it made her dizzy with joy to think that she was a part of all this, that this vast body of captured flight belonged to her, in some way – and Guido had noticed that, of course, because in those days he noticed everything. He had noticed, but he hadn't said a word, he'd just turned and smiled, the massed fluttering all around him like some gorgeous, eerie piece of theatre that he had created just for her. Then he had laughed, softly, but not in a way that a man laughs with a child. He hadn't treated her like that, ever. He had treated her as a grown-up. As a woman.

'You like this?' he asked.

Eloise nodded. 'Yes,' she said, a little breathless suddenly. 'It's – wonderful.'

Guido had smiled at that, but he wasn't laughing now and she knew he understood what she meant, because *he* thought it was wonderful too. He felt the same as she did about it, and he put his hand on her arm and held her a moment, as if he wanted to slow time, to make these few seconds last forever. 'It *is* wonderful,' he said. 'But it's not everyone who sees that.'

Eloise had been so happy then, with Guido's hand on her bare skin and the birds straining to fly around her. Now, however, he was far away in his own world and she didn't understand why. There was a time before and a time after, but it had to do with something more than the so-called accident and it had affected everything, not just Guido and her, but Daddy, too. It had even affected the people in the town, all their neighbours and friends who weren't neighbours and friends any more so that, now, it was as if there were two worlds, or maybe two lives. The first was brightly coloured and lit from within, the woods behind the town full of butterflies and wild birds, Guido strong and tall and mysterious, going back and forth between the town and the hills and Daddy taking his special girl out every evening for the passeggiata, the two of them known and recognised by everyone because, in those days, everyone was a friend or a neighbour or a business acquaintance of Daddy's. This life she had now, though, was pale and colourless by comparison, a life of silences and looks she didn't understand, Guido staring out into the street like a *pazzo* and Daddy little more than a shadow, hiding himself away in some dim corner of the apartment and only ever coming out when she did something wrong. It was like everything she had ever known was gone – and this third day was always a little sad because, sitting out here, waiting for her chosen boy to find her, she couldn't help thinking about what she had lost, without ever knowing how she lost it, or why. At the same time, though, it was also an integral part of the story, this third day: part of the ritual that prepared the way for what happened next and, as much as it pained her, she had to go through it. She had to go through it because it belonged, and the story would never be complete without it.

Not that it wasn't a relief, however, when her chosen boy appeared, coming home wet from the beach, say, with a rolled towel in his arms, or wandering out into the courtyard mid-morning, to kill some time while the grown-ups made lunch. This time, it was almost noon before Toby drifted out to the landing outside his apartment and stood a long moment, unsure of what to do with himself, before he noticed her smiling up at him from below. He looked awkwardly from Eloise to Guido and then back again, his expression a mix of embarrassment and apprehension and she saw that he was afraid she might do or say something cruel – which meant, of course, that he wanted, not to be left alone, but to be reassured that she was kind. Eloise let her smile brighten. '*Buongiorno*,' she called, her voice pleasing and airy. 'Did you sleep well?'

The boy nodded, but he didn't say anything.

'That's good,' she said. 'How is your father? Settling in?'

The boy's face betrayed a hint of long-accustomed disappointment before righting itself again. 'He's fine,' he said. 'He's got some work to do . . .'

'Ah! So you're on your own for a bit?'

The boy nodded again. 'For a bit,' he said. 'He'll be finishing up soon.'

'Well,' Eloise said, pretending not to see through the lie. 'I was just on my way to the market before it closes. Would you like to come along?'

The boy shook his head. 'I don't know,' he said.

'It won't be long,' she said. 'I'll show you the best place to get ice cream on the whole of the Amalfi Coast.'

The boy hesitated a moment, then he looked back in the direction of the apartment where his father was no doubt already deeply immersed in paperwork. He seemed uncertain, which meant that he wanted to come.

'It's OK,' Eloise called. 'We won't be gone for long. Then your father can take you to Ravello on the bus. It's lovely, Ravello.' She smiled happily, as if she were planning a trip there herself, though she hadn't been to Ravello, or anywhere else, for years. 'Come on,' she said. 'I'll tell you all about it.'

If the beginnings and the endings of Eloise's stories always varied, the one constant was that, every year, without fail, that third day set the pattern for those that would follow. Though she knew she only had ten days or a fortnight at most to do her work, Eloise forced herself to be patient and build up the relationship one step at a time: a walk to the beach, a conversation over an ice cream, a couple of playful Italian lessons – *gelati, grazie, prego* – till, finally, when the moment was right, she felt confident enough to invite her new friend into the apartment for lunch, or a Coke. The decisive moment was when the boy crossed her threshold; from there, it was only a short step to wine and the first mention of the roccolo. To rush things before she had won a boy's trust could ruin everything, so it was important to take things slowly and, anyway, there was an argument that said this was the happiest time of her year, this time of making friends. She enjoyed entertaining the boys, offering them cakes and pastries and then, gradually, glasses of wine, telling them stories about the animals you could see in the hills, or the strange creatures the fishermen found in their nets after a storm. It was always good to talk about animals – the boys liked that more than anything. It was like sharing a nostalgia for a place and a time that neither of them had ever really seen, but knew in their bones and at the back of their minds. To begin with, she had taken out her old photograph albums and showed the boys pictures of herself and Daddy when he was young, but they didn't want such things, it made them uncomfortable and, before long, she turned to the animal stories that Guido and others had told her, repeating them, as the years went by, with that odd mix of reverence and detachment that good storytellers always have, while she doled out cakes from Andrea's bakery and little glasses of the sweet wine that she'd selected carefully, just for them. To begin with, most refused the wine, even though she knew they wanted to try it but, after a while, they developed a taste for that chill sweetness – and that was when she knew it was time to move to the next chapter of the story. It wasn't that she was getting them drunk; it was just that this was a necessary part of the ritual, a stage in their preparation for the roccolo. They had to have that warmth inside them, that warmth of the hills and that sweetness that was so close to the sweetness of blood. After that, they were ready, just as she had been, long ago. She would talk about the old days, when she and Guido had gone out hunting, though she wouldn't mention the needle or the blinding of the eyes. Instead she would talk about tradition, and the old ways, till she judged that it was time to lead her new friend up the path that ran through the town and away to where the roccolo waited, cool and dark in the brightness of afternoon, like a tabernacle, or that tomb in the gospel where the dead are resurrected. That was the point of the story, of course, that moment in the roccolo, and she had a feeling that, this time, Toby would understand exactly what it was that she wanted him to see. What she wanted him to know. He was, after all, a lonely boy – and the lonely ones were always the best. In fact, that was what made all the difference: if only the world were populated by the lonely ones, and nobody else, things would be a good deal better for it.

Of course, it was also easier to win a lonely boy's affec-tion – and so it proved with Toby. Eloise took him walking around the town; she let him carry her bags when she went to the market; she showed him the secret path that led up into the hills behind the old church. On the fifth day, she invited him to have a coffee at Marinelli's garden café and watched as he took hesitant sips of his latte. It was obvious that he didn't really like it, but it felt grown up to him, drinking coffee with this strange woman and, the next day, when she invited him to take lunch at her apartment, he accepted without a moment's hesitation. He did hesitate when, after he had eaten two huge bowls of pasta, she poured him half a glass of dessert wine but, a moment later, he happily drank it down and, when Eloise asked if it was good, he nodded fiercely and let her fill the glass again, this time to the brim. That was probably their happiest afternoon. Usually, when they were together, Toby would always be pulling at the collar of his shirt, to make sure his birthmark was covered up, but that day he forgot about it altogether. He talked about school, and the friends he missed. He talked about a girl who lived on his street, a slightly older girl called Suzy, or maybe Sally, and it was obvious, not only that he had a huge crush on her, but that she wasn't the least bit interested. He even talked a little about his parents' divorce, though she was careful not to push him too hard on that subject. For her part, Eloise spoke about her happy childhood and how different things had been back then. How Guido had been tall and handsome, how her father had taken her everywhere and the people they met would call her *principessa*. Then she talked about how beautiful it was up in the hills, away from all the traffic and the people, and she told the boy about her special place, a place that nobody else even knew about. Toby was intrigued by that, of course. A mysterious special place, a secret house in the woods – how could a boy resist. She didn't tell him what that special place had been built for – that could wait till later – but she promised to take him there sometime, if he thought he would like it. Of course, Toby said he would *love* it.

Still, it wasn't until the tenth day that Eloise decided that he was ready for the roccolo. There had been rain in the night, but now the sun was out and, by the time the boy appeared in the courtyard, the flagstones were dry and the sky was clear. When he saw her, he gave his usual shy smile, but she could tell he was with her now – not because he really liked her, of course, but because he thought he had won her over, after the small unpleasantness of their first meeting. Like every boy she had ever taken to the roccolo, he liked her because he thought she liked *him*. He didn't know about love and, if he had, it would have scared him away. What he wanted was to be looked at in a certain way, to be seen in a kindly light, but love wasn't like that at all. Love was a test, and if you passed that test, everything changed forever.

Eloise smiled as Toby came down the stairs to where she sat in her usual place, near the oleanders. 'Good morning,' she said. 'Did you sleep well?'

Toby nodded but, for a moment, he didn't say anything. He seemed excited, slightly breathless. 'Will you show me that place today?' he said. 'You know—'

'The roccolo?'

'Yes.'

Eloise pretended to consider for a moment. 'The track will be rather wet today,' she said, adopting a serious, almost parental expression. 'It rained in the night.'

'Not that much,' Toby said.

'But it's steep, and—'

'Please?'

Eloise let the smile return to her face. 'All right, then,' she said. She looked him up and down. 'Are you ready?'

Toby nodded happily. 'I'm ready,' he said. Eloise didn't know what it was he expected to see – she never did know – but the thought crossed her mind that, this time, everything would go smoothly. Toby would understand the meaning of the roccolo, Daddy would stay away, there would be one long moment, after they had set their trap and waited patiently for the birds to come – one long moment when the boy came with her, through the darkness and the panic of the birds, to the place she had found long ago with Guido, the place where everything stopped and the world changed forever. He would thank her for that, some day. 'Can we go now?'

Eloise nodded. 'Yes,' she said. 'We can go.'

The walk to the roccolo took almost an hour. As soon as they started up the path that led away from the town and up into the hills, Toby became excited, perhaps even overexcited, at the prospect of the climb.

'Are we going to the top?' he asked, his face eager and bright.

Eloise had to smile. He was such an innocent, and so easy to please. She noticed that, today, he was wearing an ordinary T-shirt with his camouflage trousers, and he didn't seem to mind that it revealed more of his birthmark than the collared shirts he usually favoured. 'Almost,' she said. She had climbed this same path the previous evening to get everything ready. The roccolo was in its usual state,

the old nets from Guido's time were streaked with cobwebs
and still dry, in spite of the recent rain, and the bird she
had caught a few days earlier was hanging in its cage, just
behind the door, ready to be pricked and tethered for the
hunt. 'It won't take long,' she said. 'If you get tired we
can take a break.'

Toby had his eyes fixed on the hilltop. 'I'm not tired,'
he said. 'This is fun.'

He was right, of course. It *was* fun, this walk in the
summer sunshine. Fun for the boy and, for Eloise, a quiet
pleasure, to be lingered over and savoured. There might
be a little unpleasantness later, when she pricked the bird's
eyes, and she hoped Toby would understand why it had
to be done. Sometimes a boy would react badly, and Toby
was a tender-hearted child – but she would explain, when
the time came, and she would tell him how it didn't hurt,
just the way Guido had when she first came to the roccolo.
She smiled. 'This is my favourite place in the whole world,'
she said. 'I've been coming here since I was a little girl.'

'Did you come here with your father?' Toby asked.

It was the first time he had ever put such a question
to her and Eloise knew it was a sign of the progress she
had made. They were like friends now, like equals.
'Sometimes,' she said, though it wasn't true; she had never
come here with Daddy, though there had been occasions
when he had come out here to find her. Eloise looked
up and scanned the hill, and Toby's eyes followed, an imita-
tion that was also a form of flattery. They were making
good progress but the roccolo was still a fifteen-minute
walk away. 'It's not far now,' she said.

The first thing she always noticed was the smell. Even
now, when it hadn't been used for years, the smell of birds
lingered in the nets that hung, in various states of disrepair,
around the walls. The boy noticed it too, but he was more
impressed by the darkness, and by how still it was when

they first went in. Eloise left the door open, so he wouldn't get scared – some boys were afraid of the dark, which always surprised her, because she loved it so – then she walked over to check the birdcage. Once, she had brought a pale, rather pretty boy called Sam all the way up the hill, only to find that the decoy had died in the night, and the whole game was ruined. This time, however, everything was perfect: the bird was huddled down at the bottom of the cage, trying to pretend it wasn't there, maybe hoping they would go away if it stayed quiet and didn't move. Eloise opened the door of the cage quickly and fetched it out. Then she carried it to the middle of the room, where Toby was standing, his head tilted towards the perfectly round patch of sky above.

'Look what I found,' she said. Toby looked at the bird then back to her. He seemed confused. 'It's all right,' Eloise continued, holding the bird carefully in one hand, while she removed a needle from the collar of her blouse. 'It won't hurt.'

Toby took a step back. It seemed to Eloise that he wanted to run away, but he couldn't. He was transfixed by the glint of the needle as it hovered over the bird's eye. 'No,' he said.

Eloise shook her head. 'It has to be,' she said. 'We've always done it like this.'

'What for?' The boy's voice was small and a little hoarse.

'For food,' Eloise said, quietly. 'And for love.'

Toby shook his head. 'No,' he said. He looked terrified, for the bird and maybe also for himself. 'Please don't do that,' he said.

'I have to,' Eloise said. 'It's the tradition.'

The boy closed his eyes, then he opened them again. 'Please,' he said. 'You're hurting it.'

Eloise smiled sadly. This was always the difficult part. 'It's all right,' she said. 'It won't take a minute and then you'll see—'

'But why?' Toby's voice had dropped to a whisper now, though Eloise could see that he wanted to shout at her. He wanted to shout and pull the bird from her hand and let it go free, but he couldn't. He was powerless. Eloise remembered how she had watched that first time, when Guido had taken the needle – this same needle that she was about to use – and pierced the bird's eyes, with great skill and calm, and he had made it look like a mercy. She could have fancied that the bird was glad to be used like that, with such skill and a kind of tenderness, even as it was plunged into total darkness. Of course, she knew she could never achieve that level of control. She enjoyed this moment too much and, sometimes, her hand trembled as she brought the point of the needle to the bird's eye. 'It's all right,' she said, as much to herself as to the boy. 'It won't hurt, I promise.'

They were almost there, and this time, after the difficult moment of the blinding, Eloise felt they would really make it to the best part, when everything was forgiven. And then, just as she raised the needle to the bird's wild, dark eye, everything changed. The boy was too preoccupied with the bird to notice it, of course, but Eloise felt Daddy's presence even before she saw him, his wide body looming in the narrow doorway, blocking the light. For a long moment, she refused to turn around, keeping her eyes fixed on the boy, who was staring at the living creature in her closed fist, his face working, as if he was trying to perform some difficult calculation. Then she turned to Daddy – and it was immediately obvious to her that there was something about him, something new. Maybe he'd been getting ready to go out when he'd realised Eloise and the boy were gone and he had come straight out to search for them, walking the hill track in his clean white shirt, his face newly rinsed and the smell of shaving foam about him. The smell of shaving foam, the smell of hair cream and just a hint of shoe polish. Eloise loved it when he got all dressed up to go out. He was like his old self, then, and she always wanted to go and give him a hug, to feel the new smoothness of his cheeks – but she didn't go to him, she didn't move, in fact, because she could tell that he was upset. She tried to smile at the boy, to reassure him, but his eyes were still fixed on the bird, willing her to let it go, willing the whole world to go back to how it was supposed to be.

'What did I tell you about coming up here?' Daddy said, finally breaking the quiet. His voice was low and calm, but Eloise knew he was angry with her and, almost involuntarily, she lifted her hand high above her shoulder and let the bird go, so it went skittering away against the near wall, its wings beating at the stone. At the same time, she turned back to Toby – but he still hadn't noticed Daddy, he was so caught up with the bird, his face lightening as it fluttered up towards the skylight, wings beating and flickering wildly against the wall as it tried, and failed, to fly free. She turned back to Daddy. 'I wasn't doing anything,' she said – and immediately, she was annoyed with herself for sounding so meek and whiny, like a naughty child who's just been scolded. And in fact she *had* been scolded, but it wasn't right, because she wasn't naughty, she was just telling a story, like a story in an old book, and she knew that this boy would thank her, one day, for making him part of it. 'It's not fair,' she said – and she wanted to say more, about how he always spoiled things, and how he didn't understand, but she couldn't. She just froze inside, waiting for him to answer.

Daddy didn't answer, though; not at first. He stood very still in the doorway, very still and large in a sweet aura of soap and polish. Then he shook his head and said, almost in a whisper, 'Send this boy home to his father,' – and then, after a brief pause, Eloise thought she heard him say something else, but she couldn't make it out. She looked at Toby. He was still watching the bird as it fluttered haplessly against the walls, almost but not quite finding the skylight, and it occurred to her then that he hadn't even noticed Daddy, he'd been so caught up in his stupid pity and little-boy squeamishness. But then, what was he, after all, but a little boy? A stupid boy who couldn't understand the kind of gift she was offering him.

'Well?' she said. Her voice came out louder than she had intended, harsh and loud, almost a shout, and it startled Toby out of his reverie. He turned to her with a strange look in his eyes – a look that she could easily have mistaken for hate – but he didn't say anything. Eloise took a breath and made herself quiet again. 'You heard what he said.'

The boy looked at her stupidly, and it was obvious that he hadn't heard anything or, if he had, that he hadn't understood.

'Go on,' she said, then she turned away, so as not to see him any more. 'Go back to your father. He'll be wondering where you are.' She wasn't angry with him – this had happened too often now, for her to be angry – but, in an involuntary movement that she knew from somewhere, not just from her own memory of these moments, but from somewhere else too, her hand went up as if to strike him, and the boy turned quickly and ran out, not because he was afraid of her but out of pity, almost, as if he wanted to prevent her from making a fool of herself. He didn't speak, he didn't cry, he just ran out, hurrying past Daddy as if he wasn't even there and out into the dry heat of the afternoon. Eloise let her hand fall, then, and stood very still, listening. It was silent. Still she didn't move.

Daddy didn't move either. He didn't move and he didn't speak, but Eloise knew what he would do next, just as she knew that he didn't understand why she played this game. He didn't understand that she did it because she loved these boys, each in his own way; he thought she was being cruel, making fun of them or breaking their hearts for a while, because she was bored – and she was bored, but that wasn't the whole story and it pained her that he didn't understand her love. But then, he had never understood, because he was too sensible to love anyone like that. He was too sensible, too controlled, always watching, always catching her out at the decisive moment, just as he had done now, coming to the door and standing there, no more than a shadow in the bright sun, till the boy saw his chance and darted away to safety. Of course, they didn't understand either, those boys. They probably thought Daddy was being kind, they probably thought he was saving them from something terrible and ugly – but Daddy didn't know what kindness was. He was a creature of logic, not kindness and, now, when he finally crossed the floor of the roccolo and, in one sweeping movement, almost without even trying, gathered the frightened bird in his fist, he wasn't being kind at all, he was just following a logic that those boys could never understand. He gathered the bird in and held it for a moment, gently, so as not to harm it; then he went and stood at the very centre of the stone room, directly beneath the open roof. He didn't look at Eloise and he didn't say anything. It was as if she wasn't even there. The light fell into the roccolo and it touched him as he raised his arm and, in the same slow movement, let his fingers unfurl so the bird rose and flew straight up into the light, finding the gap in the roof unerringly as if, somehow, it had only needed his touch, his strong grip to guide it to freedom. That was what they did every time – and it always surprised her, because they had been so wild and desperate just a moment before, and it seemed that they ought to have struggled, for a moment at least, beating frantically against the stone roof before they finally slipped free. But they never did. After Daddy released them, they always knew exactly where to go, rising up into the light without a moment's hesitation and vanishing, just one last flutter of wings echoing in the cold stone well of the bird room, a sound so bright and final it was like a book being snapped shut, before silence fell and Eloise came back to herself, alone now, in the usual ruin of old netting and bird-smell and long-discarded feathers.

THE FUTURE OF SNOW

When it snows hard, I drive up to the foot of the hill-walkers' trail, two miles along the Inver road, and I sit for a while in the car park. I'm not on duty; I'm not there for a reason. I just feel like I need to take some time to myself and watch the snow falling at the end of another year, in a place where Margaret and the girls wouldn't think to look for me. I sit an hour or so, then I drive away with my head full of whiteness and quiet. I never get out of the car, though; I haven't done that for a long time, and the only reason this morning is any different is because Frank Morton is out there in his shirtsleeves, having one of his spells. That's what people call it in town, when he goes all hazy and wanders off, like some drunk on a pub crawl that everybody else has abandoned. Only, this morning, two days before Christmas, he's stone-cold sober. He always is; though he had his moments, before he was married. Everybody knew Frank back when he was single and nobody had a bad word to say about him. Now, we all turn aside when we see him on the high street, partly from embarrassment and partly because we're not sure bad luck isn't catching. *Poor Frank*, we say, once he's moved on and is safely out of earshot, and we think back to a carefree boy who never really existed: Frank before Beth, Frank before 'the accident'. Though we don't choose to dwell and the truth is that, if he disappeared for good one winter's day, nobody would mind that much.

It's my job to mind, though, being the police and all. I'd rather steer clear of him myself, for reasons the town doesn't know about, but if I see a man in just his slippers wandering the hill road in a blizzard, I have to pull over. I've had to deal with him a couple of times already, when I've found him out wandering the streets at night in his shirtsleeves and a pair of old moccasins. He's never any trouble though and, afterwards, if I see him on the street, he looks straight past me, like he doesn't remember a thing.

This morning, it's that blue and red striped shirt he's wearing, the jazzy one. I was there when Beth bought it, a week before she died, so I know why he's wearing it today, for this anniversary. That shirt was the last thing she ever gave him, a present he must have found under the tree and unwrapped by himself in an empty house, turning the package over and over, searching for some lingering trace of scent or touch in the wrapping and hoping it would bring her back, somehow. Maybe she had a gift for me, too, but I never received it. Probably it was there, in the car, all the time we were recovering her body from the snow. Frank didn't report her missing till it was too late, which is odd, considering. Usually, he liked to know where she was and what she was up to, which made it hard for us to see each other, and we were careful to cover our tracks along the way. Sometimes I wonder if he found that present afterwards, and wondered who it was for. It wouldn't have been a shirt, or anything like that. It wouldn't have been anything she might have given him, so he must have been puzzled by it. I like to think about that present sometimes. I imagine it was a book, or maybe a CD. She loved music, and she was always trying to get me to listen to some new thing that she had discovered, some jazz record on the ECM label, say, or a sampler of throat singing from Mongolia or Labrador.

Now, I draw up alongside him and roll down the window. He's stopped walking, though not because I'm there. What he does when he's like this isn't subject to any external logic. He's been claimed by the whiteness and the light off the snow. I switch off the ignition and the quiet hits me like a reproach.

'How's it going, Frank?' I call to him, trying not to be too loud in all this chill, empty space. It's a bit lame, but that doesn't matter, because he's staring off into the distance, not paying me any mind at all. 'Come on, man,' I say. 'You'll catch your death.'

That gets his attention. That word. Like the one word you know in a foreign language. *Death*. He's been thinking about death for two years, more or less non-stop, I imagine. First Beth's, then his own. He turns to me – and I'm certain, during those first few seconds, that he has no idea *who* I am.

'Get in the car,' I say. 'I'll take you home.'

He shakes his head but it isn't a refusal. It's more like wonder, and it occurs to me that the very *idea* of home seems absurd to him. Like heaven, or the land of the fairies. I give him a moment to get his head around the notion, then I try again.

'Come on,' I say. 'You'll not find anything out here.'

He considers that for a long moment; then he nods, almost imperceptibly. I nod back. I don't really want him in the car and I've got no business talking about what he might or might not find out here in the snow, but what else can I do? Leave him out there to freeze, just as his wife froze, two Christmases back? That really isn't something I want on my conscience, though there was a time, before Beth died, when I would gladly have let him go to hell exactly as he pleased.

When he gets in, he doesn't do any of the usual stuff that anyone else would do, getting into a car out of the cold. He doesn't shake the gathered snow off his shirt and hair, or bang his boots against the sill, he just climbs into the passenger seat and sits there, staring out at the empty road. 'God, man,' I say, trying to keep it light and normal. 'You must be frozen.'

He looks at me then, and for a moment I think he knows something. He doesn't though, it's just me imagining the worst. He doesn't know what happened, or why and, to tell the truth, he barely even knows who I am. Though we've both lived here all our lives, we never had much to do with one another, and he's probably forgotten the three or four occasions when I've driven him home after a concerned citizen called him in, a madman in the dark, wandering around in his baffies. Now, as far as he is concerned, I'm just a man, doing his job. He doesn't know me, because he doesn't know *anybody*. *Poor Frank*, we all say, *he's depressed, he's not well*. But then, why wouldn't a man be depressed if his wife was found dead from exposure, just a few hundred yards from her car, in a place where she had no business to be? Wouldn't any man grieve for that and, at the same time, wouldn't he ask himself all the questions, alone in the wee small hours, going through the possible scenarios and trying to pick out the one that made sense, or maybe just the one that hurt him least? He's been thinking about that for a long time, but his thoughts, wherever they travelled, haven't come round to *me*. He doesn't know whose fault it is, that his wife is dead. He still hasn't worked out why she was out here, because he doesn't want to come to the obvious conclusion. He wants to keep Beth intact, now that he has lost her forever.

I start the engine. 'OK,' I say. 'Let's get you home.' And though I'm the one who's sane, though I'm the one in charge, I can't help feeling like a fool when I talk to him. A fool, or maybe a guilty child, trying to cover up what he's done.

He doesn't look at me, but I know he's heard. He's thinking. He's going through a long sequence of thoughts and memories that he can't quite fit together and he has no idea that I'm the one who can make it all fall into place. He'll never know. I want to keep Beth intact too, and the Beth I'm thinking about isn't the one he remembers. Finally, he puts his puzzle aside, quietly, deliberately, the way my mother used to put away her knitting when somebody came to the door. Drops of snow and meltwater fall from his hair on to his sodden shirt. 'It's nearly Christmas,' he says suddenly.

I nod. 'Almost,' I say.

His face changes, but I'm not sure what's happening. At first I think he's smiling, but then it looks like a smothered howl. 'White Christmas,' he says, finally.

'White Christmas,' I repeat, for no reason.

He looks at me. 'So they got it wrong,' he says. 'There's still snow after all.' He waits for me to agree, but I don't know what he means, and I turn back to the road. I have a sudden image of Beth, the day we found her at the foot of the drop, half-hidden in snowdrift and I wonder why she was there. We weren't supposed to meet that day, it was supposed to be Christmas Eve. The day after. The Thursday, not the Wednesday: we'd *agreed* that. Christmas Eve. I was in town, buying presents, and all the time she was out there, wandering up the path in the snow, waiting for me, I suppose. Nobody will ever know why she fell, or why she was even out of her car in the first place. Some days, we'd walk up that trail for a bit, away from the car park where somebody might see, and I suppose that was it, that was why she started walking, because she thought I was already up on the hill.

Frank is looking at me curiously now and I realise that I owe him an answer. I just don't know what it is. 'How do you mean?' I say.

He laughs softly. 'They said it was all finished,' he says. 'No more snow. No more white Christmas.'

'Who said that?' I say.

'The weather people,' he says. 'They proved it. The world's getting warmer all the time.' He looks down at his wet clothes as if he's noticing them for the first time.

'No more snow,' he says, his voice slow with wonder. We're back at the town limit now, the name almost illegible on the sign as it flashes by. I take the back roads, to avoid the high street — I owe him that small consideration — but I don't think he cares. He's thinking about the future of snow, because he doesn't want to put together the last two or three pieces of a simple puzzle that will explain everything, and all I can do for him now is hold my tongue. He's losing his mind, perhaps, trying not to hear what's unfolding in his head, and I could end that slow drift into whiteness by telling him what he needs to know, but I don't — I can't — because the story I could tell him is too ordinary. It's not some big romance, it's not some drama out of the operas that Beth liked so much, it's just something that happened, a game we played to ease the boredom of living in a town like this, and the disappointment of being the people we turned out to be.

When I get to Frank's house, at the end of a street where every other window has a tree, I see it's dark, like a house nobody has lived in for months, or years. I pull over. 'Will you be all right?' I ask, though I already know the answer.

He doesn't say anything. He just sits a moment, staring at the house. Then, finally, he opens the door. 'How will we ever find her,' he says. 'When there's no more snow?' He hovers a moment over the thing he wants to say and can't put into words, then he gets out of the car. The seat is wet where he was sitting and I wonder if I should see him safely inside, but I don't. Instead, I start the car as soon as he is gone, and I'm pulling away by the time he reaches his front door. I want to go back, to drive out along the Inver road and see if Beth is there, walking in the snow, the way he must have imagined her, but I don't do that either, because Margaret and the girls will be starting to think about lunch, and they're probably wondering where I am.

ACKNOWLEDGEMENTS

'Something Like Happy', 'The Bell-ringer' and 'The Cold Outside' were first published in the *New Yorker*.

'Slut's Hair' was first published in the *Sunday Times*.

'Peach Melba' was commissioned for the anthology *À Table*, published by Metailié, of Paris; first English publication was in the *Guardian*.

'Perfect and Private Things' was first published in the *New Statesman*.

'The Deer Larder' was commissioned by Scottish Book Trust, for their second *Jura* anthology.

'A Winter's Tale' was commissioned by the *Sunday Herald*.

'Lost Someone' and 'The Future of Snow' were commissioned and broadcast by the BBC.